The Ghosts of Now

THE GHOSTS OF NOW

"A feeling of dread begins to creep through my shoulder. Maybe it's a premonition. I don't know. I'm staring at the telephone when it rings so loudly that I jump. It takes all the courage I've got to move toward it a step at a time. It rings again as I put my hand on the receiver and the vibration trembles through my body.

'Hello?' I clear my throat and try again, speaking more loudly. 'Hello?'

The voice that comes over the phone is a whisper. 'Angie?'

In the pause that follows, I shout, 'Who is this?'

There's a strange sound, like a sob or even a smothered laugh, and the whisper continues. 'Your brother is dead.'

An anonymous phone call changes Angie Dupree's life for ever. With her brother critically ill, her fight to know the truth about that fateful night leads Angie into danger and fear. Uncertain whom she can trust, Angie begins a dramatic struggle to save her brother . . .

Joan Lowery Nixon is the author of many books for young people, including *The Stalker* which has already been published by Corgi Freeway Books, *A Deadly Game of Magic* and *The Kidnapping of Christina Lattimore* which won the American Edgar Allan Poe Award for the best young people's mystery of the year. Joan Lowery Nixon lives in Texas, U.S.A.

*Also by Joan Lowery Nixon and published by Corgi
Freeway Books:*

THE STALKER

The Ghosts of Now

Joan Lowery Nixon

CORGI
F·R·E·E·W·A·Y

THE GHOSTS OF NOW

A CORGI FREEWAY BOOK   0 552 52371 2

Originally published in U.S.A. by Delacorte Press 1984

First publication in Great Britain

PRINTING HISTORY

Corgi Freeway edition published 1987

This book is set in 11/12pt Paladium.

Corgi Freeway Books are published by Transworld Publishers Ltd:,
61-63 Uxbridge Road, Ealing, London W5 5SA, in Australia by
Transworld Publishers (Australia) Pty. Ltd., 15-23 Helles
Avenue, Moorebank, NSW 2170, and in New Zealand by Transworld
Publishers (N.Z.) Ltd., Cnr. Moselle and Waipareira Avenues,
Henderson, Auckland.

Printed and bound in Great Britain by
Cox & Wyman Ltd, Reading

*with love to
Amy Berkower,
a special friend*

CHAPTER ONE

You can make it, Angie, I tell myself. *Hey! You're a good kid. You'll survive.* I clench my teeth and stare through the dusty classroom window. Across the street squats a row of ancient houses with brick the color of mud, wisps of lawn, and scraggly, parched trees. I think of the old cliché "What's a nice girl like me doing in a place like this?" and I have to smile, in spite of the way I feel. I've survived before.

Maybe I'm in this mood because the other places we've lived have had something going for them, and this place doesn't. Maybe it's because of the uneasy feeling I've had about this town from the moment we climbed off the plane, knowing this town would be our new home. Mom said later that all she could see were those flat stretches of dusty mesquite, but I saw the faces — some of them weathered like old shoes, some of them squinting against the blowing sand, some of them curious as they glanced at us, some of them suspicious, and none of them friendly.

Five minutes until the bell will ring on my first day in senior English in this stupid high school in this stupid town, and I sit here pep-talking myself. Meredith would have a good laugh at that. I'll write and tell her all about it and about the girl with the capped teeth who's sitting in the row next to me and how I said "Hi" and her glance flicked off my forehead the way a June bug bounces off a lighted windowpane before she turned away. Great school. Friendly kids. I have to stop thinking of Meredith or I'll start to cry.

A hand gently touches my shoulder, tearing me from my thoughts so abruptly that I jump.

"I didn't mean to scare you," a deep voice says in my right ear. "I just wanted to say howdy."

He's tall and lean with a sunburned nose and light brown, curly hair. He's got a grin right out of a soft drink commercial and an accent so broad that his words sound spread out and buttered. "Del," he says. "Del Scully."

"Angie Dupree."

He leans over his desk, elbows jutting into the aisles, his face close to mine. "You gotta be new to Fairlie. I'd remember if I'd seen you around school before this." He pauses and adds, "Your eyes are the darkest blue I've ever seen, Angie. They're really something on a blonde."

Just like a kid I start to blush, and he grins again at my embarrassment.

"So what are you doing in West Texas?" he asks. "Your daddy with an oil company?"

I answer with a nod while I say to myself, *That's a good question. What am I doing in a place like Fairlie, Texas? What have I been doing all my life, moving to new cities and new schools and saying good-bye to friends and hello to strangers, swallowing tears and wishing I were somewhere else while my father moves up and up something he calls the corporate ladder?*

"Tough," he says.

"What?" For a moment I think he's reading my mind.

But one side of Del's mouth twists into a rueful smile as he says "A lot of folks don't like the oil companies coming in to suck out all those big bucks."

"It's not my fault! It's not the oil companies' fault.

10

Those people shouldn't have bought their land without the mineral rights." It comes out angry, but Del puts a hand on my shoulder.

"Hey! I'm glad you're here. Where are you from?"

"Los Angeles, this time."

"Disneyland," he says.

I giggle. "I didn't exactly live there."

"I've never been. Tell me about it." A short woman, trying to balance a stack of papers, steers a zigzag course from the front door to her desk, and the room quiets. Del mumbles, "Talk to you later," and manages to fold his long legs in their scuffed cowboy boots under his desk.

It's like any other new day in a new school. The ins versus the outs, and these ins are easy to spot. Friendly old Capped Teeth is in, but she's a follower. Someone named Debbie, who's an impression of pink and white and lots of money and *has* to be a cheerleader, seems to be the center of a lot of flutter and flatter.

I find that I'm ahead in my reading in English, but their French teacher is tougher than the one I'd had, and chemistry isn't going to be any snap. Never mind. My grades are good because I'm willing to work for them. I can stand this place for one year — just one. Then Meredith and I will room together at the University of Southern California. Back to California and a friend I'm going to keep. Dad promised if I'm accepted I can go. And I will be. No doubt about it, because that's my goal.

I walk home from school. It's just six blocks. Mom picked out a big home facing a pocket park. Somehow it looks like all the other homes we've lived in. Change the sofa, change the bedspreads, add some decorator touches here and there, but they still look alike. They just keep getting a little larger,

11

and a little more important looking.

"This will be your room, down the hall from Jeremy's," Mom had said when she first showed me through this house and opened the door to a large bedroom with its own bath and with wide windows facing the garden.

But it isn't my room. My room is in my imagination. It's a dorm room with everything that's important to me stuffed into my side of the closet so I won't crowd into Meredith's space. For now it's my daydream room. But just a year until I get there. Just a year until it's mine.

I unlock the front door, grateful for the rush of cooled air, and wander through the entry hall to the dining room, dropping my books on the table. "I'm home, Mom," I shout.

Jeremy comes through the door to the kitchen, stuffing the ragged remains of a sandwich in his mouth, saying "She's not here."

About a year ago my little brother got to be as tall as I am, and now he's about two inches taller — around five-ten. He eats all the time and it doesn't help. He's still skinny.

Jeremy has his head cocked now, his eyes on mine. "This school is dumb," he says.

"So are all tenth graders," I answer, pushing past him into the kitchen. "Anything good to eat in here?"

"Chocolate chip cookies," he says, following me. "I mean nobody's friendly." He stops and looks at me again. "Are they?"

"No, they're not."

He folds himself into the nearest chair and relaxes against the kitchen table. He shoves a ragged Monopoly box toward me. "Look what I found in that box of books Mom told me to unpack."

I grin, thinking about the wild Monopoly games

12

Jeremy and I played with each other as we were growing up. "I used to get so mad at you when you'd beat me!"

He rubs his shoulder. "I remember!"

"Look, I only socked you once."

Jeremy pushes the box aside. "There's a guy named Boyd in my P.E. class. They matched us as tennis partners. He says most of the kids have lived here all their lives. They don't have much to do with the oil people. Or the farmers. They call the farmers 'kickers'."

I shut the refrigerator door with one elbow and carry my glass of milk and fist of cookies to the table. "Who cares?"

"Nobody." Jeremy reaches across the table for one of my cookies, and I move them with one hand, giving him an arm chop with the other. "I just wanted one," he says, rubbing his arm. When I don't answer he adds, "Have you seen those kickers? They all wear cowboy hats and boots and jeans, and a lot of them drive pickup trucks."

I think of Del. I didn't see him after class was over. Maybe I would like to tell him about Disneyland. Maybe I will.

"I'd like to have boots." He thinks about that for a minute. "Boyd says that a lot of those guys come right to school from the barn. He doesn't like them."

"Who's this guy Boyd? Another loser like your friend George in L.A.?"

I wish I hadn't said it. That was mean. I keep telling Jeremy that he shows he's too eager to make friends; so naturally everywhere we go he gets the leftovers, the sort of odd people no one else wants. But it doesn't do any good. And just because I'm in a rotten mood myself I've hurt him. I didn't mean to.

He sits up tall, trying to look as though what I

13

said couldn't possibly matter. "I told you, Angie. Boyd is my tennis partner. We're pretty evenly matched, and probably the best of the tennis teams. I might even end up with a tennis scholarship when I graduate."

"Great." I attempt to sound more enthusiastic than I feel. "Speaking of college, if I want to get there I'd better study. You too."

"Don't try to be my mother," he says. Then he shrugs and mumbles, "Yeah. Why not study? There's nothing else to do."

I find myself saying "Unless you'd like to try just one more game of Monopoly. This time I'm going to beat you."

The game doesn't last long. Jeremy puts enough hotels on Indiana to create a convention center, and of course I land on it, which wipes me out.

Jeremy heads for his room, laughing like the fiend on the late late show. I stop to rinse out my glass and hear the back door open. "Mom?"

There's a stumbling sound, and Mom mutters something under her breath. The door from the utility room to the garage slams. I put down my dish towel and go to meet her. "Got something to carry?"

"No, no," she says. She leans against the washing machine and makes an effort to focus on me. "Honey," she says, spacing her words, "how did it go at school today?"

"You need some coffee." The chill in my voice must have touched her, because she shivers.

She tries to sound lighthearted. "Oh, I'd love a cup of coffee. And you can tell me all about the new friends you've made."

I take her elbow and guide her into a kitchen chair. "Mom, you're talking to me as though I'm in the third grade."

She sits at the table, shoulders hunched, staring at her hands, which are resting in front of her. Her blond hair may be touched up, but it's swirled into the latest hairstyle, and the cosmetics that give her a polished glow are the most expensive on the market. The day is sticky with stale, dragged-out summer heat, but in spite of the temperature and of having too much to drink, Mom still looks crisp and cool. She's beautiful, and occasionally, when her acquaintances gush that I look like my mother, I really don't mind a bit.

As I put coffee in the filter and pour water over it she raises her head and says, "You're good at making friends, Angie. With every new school you always come home and tell me about your friends."

"When I was little."

"Not just then, honey. What about that Marilyn you were always with in Los Angles?"

"Meredith."

"Sure. Meredith." She hiccups.

The coffee's ready, so I bring her a cup and sit opposite her. She cradles the cup between her hands and smiles at me. "Mom," I ask, "why did you drink too much?"

"It's those bloody Bloody Marys." She giggles into her coffee cup until the heat of the liquid stops her. "I mean," she finally says, "that they taste like jazzed up tomato juice, so if I have a couple or three I don't know it's too many until it's too many."

"Then don't have any."

"It helps. You can't im-imagine how much it helps. Oh, ho, ho, ho, there are things I could tell you." She picks up the cup again, as though she's forgotten what she was talking about, and closes her eyes as she sips.

I quickly get out of my chair. "I've got to study,

Mom. If you want me to make dinner, just tell me what to do." I don't want to hear about her problems. I've got enough of my own.

Mom doesn't answer. Never mind. She'll sleep it off in her bedroom, and when it's close to the time Dad is due home, I'll poke around in the refrigerator and find the chicken or ground round or whatever she had in mind. Dinner will be on the table, with Mom showing up looking great, as usual. She'll give me a hug and tell me I'm wonderful, and that's all we'll ever say about it.

The telephone rings, and I pick up the kitchen extension. In how many cities, how many times have I grabbed for the phone hoping it would be someone who wanted to be a friend, only to hear the same cheery voice saying "Hi! I'm with Welcome Wagon."

But this time the voice is deep, and it drawls, "Angie Dupree, I hope?"

I take a quick breath, steadying myself. When I answer, my voice is just as calm as his. "This has got to be Del. Right?"

"Yep," he drawls. "You've got a good memory for voices."

"That must be it." I can't help smiling.

"Our conversation got interrupted," he says.

"That's right. Where were we? Disneyland?"

"Don't I wish," he says. "I thought maybe I could come by your place tonight, if you're not too busy. It's going to stay light until around eight. I can bring the pickup and show you around Fairlie."

"I'd like that," I answer. He tells me he'll come "after supper," around six thirty. I put down the receiver, lean against the counter, and grin. The grand tour of Fairlie, in a pickup truck. I wish I could tell Meredith about that.

At twenty after six Dad comes in the door, drops

16

his briefcase on a chair, pulls off his suit jacket, and yanks at his tie, all in one smooth motion. He's tall and trim, with thick brown hair, and even when he's rumpled he carries it off as though everyone's supposed to look that way.

He says, as he always does, "How did everything go today, Angie?" and "Where's your mother?"

I always say "Fine" in answer to the first question, because he doesn't hear me. Mom always comes in at this moment, and he always looks at her as though he's just won first prize in a raffle and says something like "Well, L.A. called, and I've got the raise" or "The Kenneths want us to come to dinner Friday" or "I've got to fly to Denver tomorrow."

And it goes like that now, only Jeremy rushes into the room, bumping and banging against one of the chairs as he tries to manage his long legs. His voice is a little high-pitched, as it gets when he's excited. "Boyd's stopping by tonight," he said. "I called and asked him if he could, because I want him to meet you, and he said he might, and then he said he would, and—"

"Calm down," Dad says. He puts a hand on Jeremy's shoulder.

Jeremy takes a gulp of air, nods his head, and continues. "Boyd's my tennis partner. He's good, Dad."

"Great," Dad says. "I'm counting on you to be a winner."

"I think we can win," Jeremy says. "It's going to take a lot of practice, though."

I break in and say, "Listen, everybody. Dinner's in the oven, and I've already eaten."

Mom looks as though I'd said I was running a fever. "Why did you eat by yourself?"

"Because I'm going to be taken on a tour of Fairlie." It comes out with a giggle.

17

They're staring at me, waiting for me to explain, when the doorbell rings. Naturally, Jeremy reaches the door first. "It's Boyd!" he yells and flings it wide. I wish he weren't so eager. Mom and Dad don't seem to notice, but I do, and it hurts.

But it isn't Boyd. Del steps through the door, pulling off the kind of broad-brimmed, high-crowned felt western hat I'd seen a lot of around Fairlie. He's even better-looking than I'd remembered, and I know if Meredith were here she'd groan and say, "Why'd you have to find him first?" He sticks out his right hand and shakes Jeremy's, saying "Howdy. I'm Del Scully."

Jeremy's mouth is open. "Howdy — uh — hi," he stammers.

Dad's tall, but Del looks down on him a couple of inches as I introduce him to my parents. "Welcome to Fairlie," Del tells them.

"Thank you," Dad says. He's very much the poised executive and studies Del as though he's applied for a job. "Won't you sit down?" he asks.

"That's mighty nice of you to ask," Del tells him, "but I want to show Angie around Fairlie before the sun goes down."

"I'd like to get better acquainted, to learn something about you and your family," Dad says.

But Del just grins again. "That would take hours and hours. Y'all will hear about us some day when we can stretch out our legs and take plenty of time."

At first I think he's matching Dad cool for cool, but then I realize Del's just being open and honest. He doesn't know that Dad's maneuvering to take command.

Mom hasn't said much. She just smiles kind of weakly and says, "Well, do have a nice drive." She walks with us to the front door and takes a long look at Del's dark blue pickup with the dent in the right front fender; her perfectly matched eyebrows get somewhat out of alignment.

"I'll take good care of Angie, and bring her home about ten," Del tells them. He takes my elbow and steers me down the steps, the walk, and into the front seat of his pickup truck.

As he drives away from the curb I say, "I've been wondering what there is to see in Fairlie."

"I'm going to show you some things that will make you feel more at home here," Del says.

At first I don't believe him, but I change my mind. Because what Del shows me are people. He gives me stories, not statistics; minds, not monuments.

He drives to an older part of town, where the blocks are lined with huge, brick homes set well back from the street. "This is old Judge Wallaby's house," he says, as he slows by a white-brick corner home. "The judge had a daughter whose husband just seemed to go loco and beat that little woman something awful. So she ran home to her daddy, and when the husband came after her, the judge got down his rifle and shot him dead. Shot right through that front door."

"How awful. Did the judge go to prison?"

"Nope. Nobody blamed him. It didn't even get to the grand jury."

"You mean because it was self-defense?"

"Well, sure, but also because Judge Wallaby's family helped settle this part of West Texas and build Fairlie. That son-in-law wasn't even from around these parts."

He drives to a huge yellow monstrosity on the next street, where it dead-ends near a gully. Overgrown, dusty shrubbery twists with scraggly trees in a tattered screen that hides much of the house. Here and there a window appears like an unblinking glass eye. "That's the Andrews place. Miz Andrews had so much money she didn't know what to do with it all, and after she died eight years ago every cousin and kin who ever heard her name wanted it."

"But the house looks empty. Don't any of her relatives live in it?"

"Maybe some of them will after the court finally settles things. Until then nobody wants to live there except the ghost."

I turn to stare at him, but he looks serious.

"I'm not kidding. Something moves around in there at night. The neighbors have heard it. And they've seen flickering lights."

"Have you?"

"Nope. But we might go looking sometime."

We drive until the sun explodes into scarlet shatters across an orange-streaked sky and drops beyond the flat horizon, and I hear about the people who fought the dust storms to raise cattle and scratch out farmland and cluster together in neighborhoods until one day they formed a town. Oil was discovered and Fairlie expanded, with two country clubs and twenty Baptist churches and four indoor shopping malls and all the people who kept the whole thing running.

We stop at a brick building that looks purple in the garish green light from the neon sign over the door. Inside are guys and girls in jeans and cowboy hats, and lots of them look our age. Country-western music is blaring from the juke box, and a few couples are dancing close, elbows out, feet doing a fast shuffle. Some of the kids call out to Del, and he grins back at them, at the same time gripping my right elbow again and steering me in a zigzag course into a chrome and plastic chair. He hooks the heel of his boot into the spindly leg of another chair, dragging it to a spot next to mine. While I'm busy staring around the room, a waitress slaps down two large colas.

"This is where I like to hang out," Del says. He's watching me to see how I'll react. Will it matter to him? This is a strange world to me, and I feel a little apart from it. But there's something I like about it. At the moment I wouldn't mind belonging.

"It's nice." I lean back in my chair, relaxing, and smile at him.

The question in his eyes slides from the corners into laugh crinkles. He puts a hand over one of mine and says "I'd like you to meet some of my friends."

"Okay."

"But not now. Tonight I want to find out about Angie Dupree."

It's easy to tell him about the girls' school in Los Angeles where I met Meredith, and about the fun we had together, and the surfing at Malibu and the window-shopping in Beverly Hills and the classes at the county art museum on Wilshire. But it was another planet. It was another Angie. Here, in Fairlie, Texas, a country-western singer nasally wails for a lost love, and Del's fingers are warm and strong.

He sits up, shoving back his chair with a screech along the wooden floor. "Quarter to ten," he says. "Time to get you home."

"It's still early." I don't want to go.

"I said 'ten' to your daddy. Let's get moving."

It's been a strange evening. Everything from haunted houses to country music, with a guy who seems to belong in an old-fashioned western TV show. As we drive back to my home I ask myself if this makes me like living in Fairlie any better. Maybe, for the moment. But that other world is

21

waiting. One year, and I'll be back.

There's a low, black sports car parked in front of our house. Del says, "Looks like you've got company." He walks me to the front door, says "See you tomorrow, Angie," turns, and leaves.

I don't know what I expected, but this wasn't it. What's with this cowboy's code? Doesn't he kiss girls good night? I might not have kissed him anyhow. But at least he could have tried!

I shut the front door a little harder than I mean to. The voices in the living room stop, so I hurry to let them know it's just me, and not a door-slamming burglar.

Happiness is a golden gleam in Jeremy's eyes. "Angie, this is Boyd Thacker."

Everyone in the room smiles with the same pleased expression. Everyone but Boyd. For a few moments his appraisal of me is penetrating and unblinking. Then he smiles with a polished charm that matches his dark good looks as he says "You've got a beautiful sister, Jeremy."

I don't say anything, so Mom giggles and says, "We agree."

And Dad asks me, "How was your little sightseeing tour?" Not waiting for an answer, he turns to Boyd and says, as though it's a private joke, "Angie seems to have found an honest-to-goodness cowboy."

"Kicker," Jeremy says with authority. He looks at Boyd. "I think they got that name because of the boots."

Boyd doesn't respond. He's still staring at me. He's not much taller than I am and almost as thin as Jeremy. There shouldn't be anything menacing about a person like that. But the intense look in his eyes makes me think of a snake hypnotizing a bird. I shudder.

"That air conditioning must be blowing right on

you," Mom says. "Come in here and sit down. It's pleasant in here."

So I perch on the end of the chair closest to my mother and wonder why I'm the only one who feels that there's something very wrong about Jeremy's small, dark-eyed friend.

CHAPTER TWO

After a few minutes of very dull conversation Boyd mutters something about stuff he has to do. Jeremy, trailing Boyd like an adoring puppy, goes out with him to admire his car. "Boyd's sixteen," he says, with the same awe reserved for someone who's just won the Indianapolis 500.

The door shuts, and Dad says, "His father's an attorney. I've heard of him. Very influential in Fairlie."

"Wow!" I say. "That makes him practically perfect, just like Mary Poppins."

Mom, who has been busy plumping up the cushions on the satin-striped sofa, straightens and stares at me. "I don't understand the sarcasm, Angie. Boyd seems like a nice boy to me."

"I think he's a creep," I answer. "And I don't think what his father does for a living makes any difference."

Dad leans back in his chair, making a church steeple of his fingers and resting his chin on them. He does this a lot when he's having what he calls "an important talk" with Jeremy or me, and I think it's because there's a dimple in his chin that quivers when he gets upset about anything, and this way he can cover the dimple and not give his feelings away. I bet he does that in his office too.

"Many young people are idealists," Dad says, "so I don't fault you for that, Angie. But as you grow older and become more experienced with the ways of the world, you'll find that a man's position in life does make a difference."

"A difference in what?"

His lips turn up in the barest of smiles. "Don't you think that an attorney would command more respect than — let's say — a cowboy?"

Sometimes I like to get into a good argument with my father, and we sharpen our wits against each other as though they were little knives, darting, pricking, slicing — but never very deeply. Tonight I'm not in the mood, so I say, "That's a hard question. Perry Mason versus The Lone Ranger. I'll have to give that one a lot of thought."

I get up and stretch, yawning loudly with my mouth wide open, knowing that will irritate Dad too.

The door bangs and Jeremy's in the room. "Angie, that's some kicker you came up with. He's a nice guy, though. I'd like a hat like his, except I couldn't wear it, because people would think I was trying to be a kicker. Does he ride a horse?"

"Probably," I answer. "We didn't talk much about him. He just asked a lot of questions about me."

"You just talked about yourself all that time? You sure are conceited!"

I throw a punch toward his shoulder, and he jumps out of the way, grinning. "I didn't just talk about myself. Del told me a lot of neat stuff about the people who built this town, and showed me things, like the house with ghosts in it."

Jeremy perks up. "Real ghosts?"

"How can ghosts be real when they're unreal? No one believes in ghosts." I turn to Mom and Dad and add, "Del told me some of the history of this town."

My mouth is open, ready to share some of the stories, but Jeremy interrupts. "Boyd was only here about twenty minutes, but I'm glad he came, so all of you could meet him. He's real popular at school. We're going to get in some extra practice at the courts at the country club. They're better than the courts at school, Boyd says."

I don't want to hear another word about Boyd, so I blow kisses to my parents and say, "Good night. I'm going to read over my French assignment in bed."

Mom comes to hug me and murmurs, "That cowboy *is* good-looking, dear. I'm sure he'll be just the first of lots of good-looking boys you'll meet here."

Subtle as a cement truck. I dutifully kiss her cheek, then head for my room. Later, it's hard to concentrate on French. I find myself smiling at memories of the evening, until I give up, slide under the covers, and turn out the light. And for the first time in weeks I'm able to fall asleep.

For the next few days I study during most of my spare time. I'll be at USC in less than a year. Nothing's going to stop me.

It's good to see Del every morning. He talks to me about his family, and he asks about mine. I find myself telling him things I haven't thought about for years, like when I was six and learned how to swim, then tried to teach Jeremy in the bathtub. And the time I wanted to visit Grandma; so I packed my favorite doll and a jar of peanut butter, took Jeremy by the hand and set out on a journey that ended at the police station, where we got cherry lollipops. Maybe because Del's got such an easy way about him, maybe because he never seems to be pretending like most people do, I feel comfortable with him. I think I'm beginning to trust him.

He asks me for a date for Saturday night. "You need to learn country-western dancing," he says. "And I'm the one who can teach you."

"How about disco?" I ask. "Can you dance disco?"

He shrugs. "Sure. But it's nicer up close."

I find out that Jeremy was right about Boyd being popular. He's one of the class officers and a good student, and he keeps that charm going strong. Even the teachers like him.

"Hi, Angie," he beams at me as we pass in the hallway.

I mumble something, a little embarrassed that I don't like him. I seem to be the only one who distrusts that charm, and maybe I'm wrong.

A couple of the girls in my classes begin to talk to me. Both of them have fathers with oil companies, but they've moved here years ago and feel so comfortably settled that they can talk about Fairlie like smug mothers reciting the adorable faults of their children.

"Wait till you find yourself in a sandstorm," one of them says. "It's awful. It blows through the cracks in the windows and gets on everything."

"Even in your teeth," the other says, her braces flashing. "And it howls — the wind that is."

"When are the sandstorms?"

"The wind will start soon. I know it always blows down our Christmas decorations every year."

"But the sand blows in the spring. And it goes on and on until you want to scream."

Later I ask Del about it.

"Just parts of Oklahoma wanting to come down to Texas," he says. "It's not as bad as it used to be before there was so much planted. The early farmers had it bad."

It isn't that great now, I think, and I wonder why anyone wanted to try to grow things in hard, dry, desert country like this. Not a lake or a river as far as the horizon. The town's an oasis, with spreading gray-leafed oaks like giant straws, sucking up moisture from deep below the dusty surface of the earth.

I'm paired with Debbie Hughes for a few moments during basketball practice in P.E. We've passed each other dozens of times in the halls and going in and out of classes, but this is the first time she's actually looked at me. It's an appraisal. She's sizing me up as though I were competition. Surely, not for Debbie Hughes. We're not even in the same world.

She drives a pale blue foreign car, and I've never seen her alone in it. I've never seen her alone anywhere. Even when she sweeps down the school hallways, she's in the middle of giggles and gush.

A whistle blows, a ball comes fast, and that's it. Not a word spoken. In a few minutes she's back with her own group. I don't care about Debbie. I don't care about any of them. I only care about Meredith and USC and the life I'm going to have next year.

Mom joins a study club and signs up for season tickets to the community theater. She goes to a couple of luncheons at the country club and once can't make it to dinner. "Tell your father I may have a virus," she mumbles and skips the coffee to sleep it off.

I don't think Dad's dense. I think he has too much on his mind to notice things he ought to notice. He works long hours, brings home stacks of papers to read, and occasionally grumbles to Mom about problems with his job.

"There's a lot of antagonism against the oil people in certain quarters here," he says to Mom. "It occasionally adds unnecessary problems."

Mom just shrugs and says, "Cash in hand is always the bottom line, isn't it?"

"I wouldn't want someone else to be getting the mineral profits from my land. I know how those people feel."

"We're just innocent bystanders," Mom tells him.

28

"Why should they get mad at us?"

I start to tell them about the way it is at school, with people divided into groups, with the ones like Debbie calling themselves "socialites," and the kickers, and the kids of the oil company people, but Dad sort of looks over my shoulder and murmurs "Um-hum" once in a while, so I know he's not listening. His body's home, but his mind is off somewhere else.

Jeremy comes and goes, usually with a tennis racket under his arm. He's out a lot in the evenings, and I'm surprised that's okay with Mom and Dad, but if they don't care, then why should I? Sometimes Jeremy's quiet and keeps to himself, and sometimes he rattles on and on about a lot of stuff, but I don't usually listen. It's not important. And I've got to catch up in French. He's stopped talking about Boyd Thacker so much, and that's a relief.

So the days crumble into another Friday, and that's when it's bad. On Fridays Meredith and I were usually together. Sometimes we'd double date, or make pop-corn and watch the late movie.

This Friday evening I'm alone.

Mom and Dad are going out to dinner with some company brass who've flown in from the Houston office. She stoops to kiss me good-bye. "I've left the number of the club by the phone in the den, if you need us," she says. She's wearing red silk and looks terrific.

"Perrier and lime for you tonight," Dad says to her.

She makes a little face and blinks her long lashes at him. "Not even a little white wine?"

"Perrier." He's smiling, but his tone is firm. "This dinner is very important for us. I don't want anything to spoil it."

"You know I only drink when I'm bored." She

29

takes his arm, cuddling up to his shoulder, and they leave. I settle down in front of the television set in my old jeans and a faded blue T-shirt and flip from channel to channel. Everything is boring. Everything is dumb.

"What are you watching?" The voice is behind me, and I jump and let out a yelp.

"You came in like a ghost! Scared me to death!"

"I thought you didn't believe in ghosts," Jeremy says.

"I don't." He's got a strange look on his face, and one corner of his mouth twitches as though he's trying not to smile. "Don't tell me you do."

"Maybe I do," he says. "Some kinds of ghosts, that is."

"I see. You're being selective in your ghosts. How about the ones in the Andrews place? You were ready to believe in those when I told you about them."

"Forget the Andrews place."

His tone is suddenly sharp and serious. Curiosity makes me needle him just a bit. "Why? Del and I just might do some ghost hunting there some dark night."

"Stay away from there," he says. "It's just a dumb old house."

I can't read the expression in his eyes. "What are you getting at, Jeremy?"

"Nothing," he says. He turns and moves toward the door. "I'm going out."

"Who with? Got a girl friend?"

"None of your business."

"Where are you going? Did you tell Mom and Dad?"

"Don't try to be my mother, Angie," he says. "I only have to tell *them* where I'm going, not you."

"I don't care where you're going."

"Good, because it's none of your business."

I turn the sound up louder after he leaves and try to get interested in an old movie. It bombed when it came out, and I can see why. I wish the phone would ring. I wish Del would call. Maybe he will if I concentrate on the telephone. I send all my energies toward that phone, screwing up my face in the effort. *Ring*, I tell it. *Ring!*

But it doesn't.

There are noises in the back of the house, and I go to investigate. I'm not really scared. It's just something to do. It sounds like a tree branch scraping the window. That's just what it is — a tree branch moving slightly in a breeze, its dry, curling leaves like withered fingers against the glass.

A breeze isn't bad. It might break the smothering, dry heat that each day sizzles up from the sidewalk and presses down from a flat sky. But as I watch those quivering leaves at the edge of darkness a feeling of dread begins to creep through my shoulders and up my neck. I step back from the window, gasping for breath. *What's the matter?*

"Hey!" I tell myself. "Don't let your imagination get out of control." But the suddenness of my voice in the silent room adds to my fright, and I scramble toward the puddles of bright light under the reading lamps in the den.

Maybe it's premonition. I don't know. I'm staring at the telephone when it rings so loudly that I jump. It takes all the courage I've got to move toward it a step at a time. It rings again as I put my hand on the receiver, and the vibration trembles through my body.

"Hello?" I clear my throat and try again, speaking more loudly. "Hello?"

The voice that comes over the phone is a whisper. "Angie?"

In the pause that follows I shout, "Who is this?"

There's a strange sound, like a sob or even a smothered laugh, and the whisper continues. "Your brother is dead."

31

CHAPTER THREE

"Who are you?" I scream, but I hear the click of some-one hanging up. "Who are you? What are you doing?"

I slowly put down the telephone and look at it as though it will have more to tell me. Was that some kind of a sick prank? It had to be. People aren't noti-fied of terrible things by voices like that. Are they?

There's a scrap of paper by the phone. It's the telephone number Mom left. I scoop it up and begin to dial, but my fingers are trembling so violently that I drop it, and my mind hasn't registered the number. Never mind. Dad said this was an important dinner, and what can I tell him? What if he and Mom race home in a panic, and Jeremy walks in the door like nothing had happened?

Jeremy was about ten the day he didn't come home after school. Mom and Dad had called the police, and they went out to look for him too. They told me to stay by the phone, so there I was when the door opened and Jeremy walked in. He was surprised that everyone was searching for him. All he'd been doing was playing baseball! I was so glad to see him, and so angry with him at the same time, that I hugged him, then shook him until he broke away, kicking me in the shins.

I steady myself by taking a couple of deep breaths. What if it were some creepy friend of Jeremy's think-ing he was being funny? I don't know any of Jeremy's friends. Any except Boyd. And I've got to find out where Jeremy is. Maybe Boyd will know. I perch on the edge of the chair by the telephone and thumb through the white pages until I find Boyd's address. My hands aren't shaking now. I'm able to dial the number, and when a voice answers I ask for Boyd.

The words are deep and slurred with sleep. "It's late, young lady. You shouldn't be calling boys at this hour."

"I'm sorry," I answer, apologizing automatically. "I'm Angie Dupree, and I'm only calling Boyd because I think he can help me find my younger brother. May I speak with him, please?"

He clears his throat and his words are stronger. "Oh, I see. And your brother is a friend of Boyd's?"

So Boyd hasn't bothered to tell his parents about Jeremy. Some friend.

"Tennis partners."

"At the high school?"

This man is driving me crazy. "Look, please may I speak to Boyd? It's terribly important."

"I wish I could help you," he says in a tone that means no such thing, "but Boyd isn't home. I believe he went to a party with some friends."

"Did my brother go with them?"

"I have no idea. If you like I'll leave a note for Boyd to call you when he gets home." He's grumbling like a bear dragged out of his cave during hibernation. *Come on, mister, it's only ten forty-five.*

"Never mind," I say. "Thanks anyway." I manage to hang up before he does.

The house moves with little creakings and rustlings of the night. I don't know any more now than I did when the whisperer phoned me. Where is Jeremy?

Another name comes into my head: Del. Maybe he'll know what to do. Again I grab at the phone

33

book, my fingers stumbling through until I find the name Scully. Only one Scully, thank goodness. It has to be Del's father.

So I dial the number, and it rings and rings. "Answer, please. Answer," I say, but no one does.

I lean back in the chair, my hands dropped at my sides, trying to relax, trying to think. If something had happened to Jeremy, who would know? The police? The hospital?

There is a hospital in Fairlie. It's a three-storied, brown-brick building on the outskirts of town. Maybe Jeremy is there. It can't hurt to call them. I don't know what else to do. But the hospital isn't listed under Fairlie. What is its name? It has to have a name. I brush back tears and breathe deeply and try to calm myself. Somehow I manage to think of the yellow pages, and there is the Lila Cookson Memorial Hospital.

I try to talk to an operator and then to whoever she switches me to. My interrupted sentences pile up like broken sticks, until finally a woman actually listens to me. I explain about the phone call I've received.

"Tell me about your brother," she says. "Describe him."

My tongue is thick and hard to move, but I do, and she answers, "Can your parents come to the hospital right away? We do have a boy here who was hit by a car a little while ago. He didn't have any identification on him. It might be your brother."

My words come out in heaves, in shudders. "Is he—? Did he—? No! Please, no!"

"He's in intensive care," she says. "The doctor will be able to tell you more about his condition."

Thank you thank you thank you. I know if I hear Mom's or Dad's voice I'll start to cry and won't be able to talk to them, so I give her the number on the scrap

34

of paper and their names and ask her to call them.

I snatch up my car keys and take our brown sedan. I know how to get to the hospital. It's one of the buildings Del pointed out to me on our tour of Fairlie. I try not to drive too fast, because I know only a small part of my mind is working. I have to get to the hospital. I have to get to Jeremy. Maybe I could have handled this better if it hadn't been for that terrible voice on the telephone.

Those words still cling to me as tightly as the West Texas dust that seeps inside my clothes, making a paste with my sweat-damp skin, and I can't shake them away. "Whoever you are," I say aloud to the whisperer, "I'm going to find you. Believe me, no matter how you try to hide, I'm going to find you!"

The hospital is a rush of cool, pine-eucalyptus air and the swish-splash of a mop on the brown vinyl floor. I stumble over the doorsill and sidle away from the mop. The wrinkled gnome using it never stops his back-and-forth motions, just raises his head enough to say "Wet floor. Watch your step."

The only person in the lobby is a pudgy, pale-haired man seated behind the reception desk. In his white coat he looks like a gigantic marshmallow. I stammer through my story, and he picks up the phone and talks in a low voice to someone. Finally he hangs up and says, "One of the nurses will be along in a minute." He shoves a clipboard toward me. "In the meantime you can fill out these forms."

The papers on the clipboard mean nothing to me. The words don't come together enough to make sense. "What are these papers? What have they got to do with me?"

"Just some stuff we need about your brother — medical insurance and all that."

I shove the clipboard back at him. "I'm not even

sure my brother is here! I'm not going to fill out anything!"

"Don't get so excited, sis. I just do what they tell me."

A nurse appears, managing to look efficient and sympathetic at the same time. She glances around the empty lobby. "Are your parents here too?"

Hot tears bubble up from my anger at the question, and she blurs and squiggles before my eyes. "Please, could I see my — the boy I was told was here?"

She hums-hums a moment, then says, "Perhaps you could identify him."

"Yes," I say. I take a long, deep breath. I've got to try to be patient.

"Come with me," she says, and I follow her through a side door and down a corridor. Finally we arrive at a room marked No Admittance, and my leader pushes through, holding the swinging door to let me inside.

It's a small room, with three cubicles containing beds and all sorts of electrical equipment and things I've never seen before. The first two beds are empty, but on the last narrow bed lies someone who seems to be hooked up to all sorts of devices. A nurse, hovering over him, blocks my way, so I squirm against the wall, edging around her. The two nurses say something to each other, but I don't listen. I'm too intent on the person in the bed.

Slowly I tiptoe to the open side of the bed, to a point where I can see the pale face of the boy who lies there. Suddenly I can hardly breathe.

"Oh, Jeremy!"

There's a satisfied sigh behind me, and the nurse who brought me here murmurs, "Well, now we have an identification for him, at least."

His left hand lies on top of the white cotton blanket. I pick it up and stroke it. It's warm, but his fingers,

36

relaxed in sleep, don't curl against mine. "Jeremy!" I call to him. "It's Angie. I'm here, and Mom and Dad will be here in a few minutes!"

His eyes are closed, his lashes light shadows against his cheeks. There's a large, purplish bruise that begins on Jeremy's forehead and spreads down the right side of his face to his jaw. His jaw is bandaged in a mummy-like swath that winds up and over his head. There's a cast on his right arm, and judging from the bulge under the blanket, there's also one on his right leg.

I straighten, still holding Jeremy's hand, and turn to the nurse on duty. The other one has gone. "He doesn't answer me."

She's checking something on a screen, making notations on a chart. But I need her to reassure me.

"Tell me about my brother. Will he be all right?"

"The doctor will be here soon," she says. "He'll talk to you about your brother."

The air is ice, and it shivers down my spine. "You're not answering my question!"

She reaches across the bed and rests a hand on my shoulder. "We're not allowed to," she says. "It's the doctor's place to discuss a patient's condition."

"I just want to know if my brother is going to live!"

"I'll get you some water," she says, "You're shaking. You ought to sit down." Her eyes soften, and she adds, "Look, honey, his vital signs are good. His pulse and blood pressure are okay."

"Thanks." I lean against the wall until the trembling goes away.

The first nurse I met here opens the door, leans into the room, and crooks a finger at me. "The police want to talk to you," she says.

Carefully I place Jeremy's hand on the bed. There's a bruise staining the back of his hand. As I look at it

I see something I hadn't noticed before. Something small and very light blue is protruding from under his thumbnail. I turn his hand, gently, and pull it out.

"What are you doing?" the nurse asks.

I hold my hand toward her. "It looks like a sliver of paint," I say. "It was under his thumbnail."

She leans toward me, touching it, turning it. "That's what it looks like, all right."

"Are you coming?" the nurse at the doorway calls.

I hold the paint sliver carefully between my thumb and forefinger and join her in the hallway, where a tall policeman is waiting for me.

"Can you tell me what happened?" I ask him.

"Hit 'n' run," he says. "No witnesses."

I hold out the scrap of paint. "This was under his thumbnail. Maybe it came from the car that hit him."

He takes a small envelope out of one of his pockets and carefully takes the paint sliver from me, sliding it into the envelope. He writes something on the envelope and puts it back into his pocket.

"Could you find the car from that?"

He just shrugs.

"Didn't anyone see the car?"

"Nope."

"But what about whoever was with him?"

There's a flurry at the end of the hallway. Mom and Dad burst through. This time the nurse is like a tug that's been left behind. Mom, her face sagging like a punctured beach ball, stops to hug me, then runs to catch up with Dad as he slams into the intensive care room.

The policeman licks the end of his pencil and holds it over the pad of paper in his left hand. "Where was your brother going to be tonight?" he asks me.

My mouth opens, but nothing comes out.

"Where did he say he'd be?"

"I don't know. I guess he told Mom and Dad, but he didn't tell me."

"Can you give me the names of some of his friends?"

"Boyd Thacker."

"And—?"

"I don't know."

"Do you know where he'd probably be? What did he like to do?"

"I—I really don't know. Maybe if you ask Mom and Dad—"

A man with thick white hair, whose stethoscope dangles over rumpled, green hospital clothes, stumps purposefully down the hall and into the intensive care room.

"I want to hear what the doctor says about my brother," I tell the policeman.

"Sure," he says.

But I stand there a moment, thinking of the questions to which I had no answers, realizing I know very little about my own brother.

CHAPTER FOUR

The doctor puts his glasses on, squeezes his face into a squint, and then takes them off and frowns at them as though they must belong to someone else. "It's a critical situation," he says. I look down at Jeremy and see my badly hurt brother, not a situation. Again I touch his hand, gaining some courage from the warmth of his fingers.

The doctor enumerates a fractured skull, what they hope will be only a temporary loss of consciousness, two broken ribs, a broken right arm, and a broken right leg. "He has a strong pulse, and his blood pressure is in the normal range. That looks good." He consults his chart and adds, "We found no trace of drugs."

Mom and Dad look at me as though I have something to tell them. "Of course you didn't find drugs!" I shout at the doctor. "Jeremy isn't on drugs."

"It's a routine test," he says. He squints again as he peers at me over his glasses, which now rest on the end of his nose. "Many young people do try drugs. You wouldn't necessarily be aware if your brother did."

"Not Jeremy."

"Of course not," Mom whispers, but she looks bewildered.

I add, "I'd know if he did. Kids know what to look for." I'm so angry at this doctor I shiver.

My mother's voice is soft, and it's hard to hear her. "Jeremy is going to be all right. Isn't he?"

"We hope so. There's no swelling of the brain and no hemorrhaging. But there are other factors. A lot always depends on the patient's own attitude, his own will to live."

"But surely—" Dad says. He doesn't finish his sentence.

In unison our gaze is drawn to Jeremy, and I snap, "Of course he wants to live!" At the same time a part of my mind is asking *How do I know what Jeremy really wants?*

"Jeremy?" Mom mewls like a kitten.

Dad puts an arm around her shoulders, giving her a little squeeze. "He's our son," he says. That's all. But the confidence in his voice seems to pump into Mom, and she slowly raises her head.

Dad's in command now, with the right kind of questions about Jeremy's care. The doctor attempts to convince him that Jeremy's in no condition to be flown to Houston to the medical center, that the safest thing to do is to let him rest, let his body begin to mend itself, and wait for him to regain consciousness.

Dad leads the doctor back into the hallway, leaving Mom and me and the nurse in the room with Jeremy. Mom's eyes meet mine. I'd like to have her hug me and tell me that everything will be all right, but instead I find myself saying, "Hey, it's going to be okay, Mom."

"Jeremy can't hear us."

"That doesn't matter for now."

"He's unconscious."

I remember once when I had the flu and fainted on the bathroom floor. I was dizzy, and wanted to call Mom. I had closed my eyes and could read the words in my head, as though my thoughts were typed on

41

lined paper. But the lines were suddenly broken, the words spilling apart, falling into a tunnel that hummed. It wasn't dreaming. It was another world, as I slid into a shattered part of my head. Is it this same kind of weird world where Jeremy is now?

"Don't cry, Angie," Mom says, and I realize that tears are running down my cheeks. I try to rub them away on the back of my hands.

Dad joins us with plans and decisions. "We'll go home now and rest," he says. "There's nothing we can do for Jeremy here."

"I want to stay," Mom says.

"You need some sleep," he tells her. "I'll bring you back here in the morning."

"I'd like to be with Jeremy until then," I say, but Dad shakes his head.

"You have school."

"Dad! Tomorrow is Saturday!"

"Let her stay," Mom says. "I'd like to know someone is with Jeremy."

"The nurse is with him," Dad says. "She knows what to do."

The nurse steps forward. "Hospital rules," she said. "Usually we allow only ten minutes each hour with a patient in intensive care." Her lopsided smile is probably intended to be conciliatory. "Your brother may be transferred to his own room by tomorrow," she says. "Then you can stay with him."

"We'll fly a neurologist in tomorrow," Dad says, as though that settles the whole thing. He propels Mom and me into the corridor, where the policeman is still waiting.

"What are you going to do to find the hit-and-run driver?" I ask him.

"Turn in my report, for one thing," he says, looking at me warily, as though he thinks I'm going

42

to pick a fight.

"And the sliver of paint."

"Sure," he says.

"What paint?" Dad asks.

"There was a scrap of paint under Jeremy's thumbnail."

"Don't prove anything much," the policeman says.

"It might have come from the car that hit him!"

"Maybe not. We don't know where it came from."

I take a step closer to the policeman and stare up at him. "Are you going to try to find the driver of the car?"

"Y'all asked me that already," he says. "That's not my job. That's someone else's department."

I let out a word I've been told never to say again. Mom gives a little sigh, and Dad frowns. "She's understandably upset," he tells the policeman. "This is a difficult time for all of us."

The officer shoves his hat back, and it leaves a red, greasy stripe across his forehead. "Sure. I guess so," he says.

I don't have time to add anything else. Dad's got a grip on my right arm and I'm practically flying down the hallway, Mom's high heels clattering like an accompanying drumroll as she tries to keep us with us.

"I'm going to find out who did it," I say, but Dad doesn't answer for a moment.

It's not until we're in the car that he says "The police will find out. What we need to focus in on for the moment is Jeremy's care. I thought of Dr. Branning." He turns to Mom, and they talk about specialists.

I can't get my mind away from that sliver of paint. Light blue. There must be hundreds of light blue cars in this place. Maybe the car came from somewhere else, driven by someone just passing through. But at least it's something to check out. It's better than wondering what happened.

And where.

In the east the dark sky is fading into a ragged smear of yellowed gray. Morning already, after a night that shouldn't have been. "Where did it happen?" I ask.

"What?" Mom's voice is startled. I've broken into their conversation, and it takes her a moment to react. "I don't know," she says. "Did the policeman tell you, Greg?"

"I didn't think to ask." His voice becomes louder, stronger. "It doesn't matter. What counts is getting Jeremy well again."

But it does matter, I tell myself.

Mom suddenly points at the garish green neon sign of an open-all-night grocery on the next corner. "I'm out of coffee," she says. "Could we stop?"

"I'll get it," I say as soon as Dad pulls up in front of the store. Mum stuffs a five-dollar bill in my hand, and I hurry into the store.

A fat woman with grease spots on her dress sits on a stool behind the counter. She stops talking to a man in overalls who is hunched over, elbows on the counter. They both stare at me.

I spot the cans of coffee on a nearby shelf, grab a familiar one, and hurry to the counter. "Here you are," I say, handing the woman my money. "I don't need a sack."

Slowly she pokes keys on the cash register. "You don't talk like you're from around here," she says. "You oil people?"

It sounds like a swear word. I just grab up the change and the coffee can and run from the store.

The morning is a blur of snatched sleep and tiptoed hospital visits. We carry our hushed tones back to the house, behaving like timid intruders afraid of stirring the shadows. It's hard to sort out my thoughts, but the shrill ring of the telephone gets through.

"I heard about your brother." Del's voice is solid and comforting. "I'm sorry, Angie. Can I help? You want me to come over?"

My first thought is to say no, but I realize that Del knows this town and the people in it. Maybe he will be able to help me. "Yes," I tell him. "I would like that."

He doesn't ask questions. He just says, "See you in a couple of minutes," and hangs up the phone.

Dad comes into the room as I replace the receiver. "Was that for me?"

I shake my head, and he pulls his flat leather car key case from his pocket.

"Dad, where did Jeremy tell you he was going last night?"

He scowls. "Out with friends. Maybe Boyd. Jeremy's with him often, isn't he?"

"Didn't he tell you? He told me you and Mom knew."

"I suppose he said something, the way kids do. It didn't seem terribly important — someone's house, a movie — I don't know." His eyes hold so much pain I wonder how he can bear it. "I wish—" he says softly, as though he's talking to himself. "I guess I didn't pay attention."

"Does Mom remember?"

"Not exactly. We had other things on our minds." He looks at me, and his tone shifts abruptly. "Don't pester your mother with questions, Angie. Barbara's in bed for a rest. She needs some sleep." He takes a step toward the door, then stops. "I'm going to the airport to pick up Dr. Branning. I'll be with him at the hospital for a while."

For just a moment I get the strange feeling that he's asking for my approval, but before I can answer, he

45

straightens, adjusts the knot in his tie, and strides toward the back door.

There are two more calls I have to make. I look up Boyd Thacker's number and dial it. I recognize the voice that answers. It couldn't be anyone else but Boyd.

"This is Angie," I say. "Have you heard about my brother?"

In the pause that follows I almost expect him to say "Angie who?" He finally answers, "Yeah." There's another pause, and he adds, "I heard he may not make it. Sorry it happened."

I clench the telephone and try to keep my voice from wobbling. "Exactly what did happen to Jeremy?"

I can't hear him, so when I yell "What?" into the phone he says it again.

"I don't know, Angie. What makes you think I should know?"

"Weren't you with him?"

"No."

"You're the only friend he's been spending time with."

"We just play tennis together. We're not exactly friends."

"Okay. I'm only trying to find out what happened to my brother. Isn't there anything you can tell me that might help?"

"Look, I already said I'm sorry it happened."

"Let me ask you again. Can you tell me anything about where Jeremy might have gone, or who he might have been with?"

"No," he says. "Nothing."

I slam down the phone, wishing the table top were Boyd Thacker's head. Is he lying to me? Why would he? I need more than ever to find out what went on last night.

After a couple of deep breaths that don't seem to

help a bit, I telephone the police station. Some slow-speaking clerk first establishes that I'm "family" to the hit-and-run victim, then drawls the information through her nose. I write it down — the corner of Avenue G and Huckleberry — and stare at it long after I've hung up the phone.

I hear a car drive up in front, so I get to the door before Del rings the bell. Without a word he puts his arms around me, and I lean against him, burrowing into the warmth of his comfort. This is the first time he's held me, and I feel guilty for wanting this instead of thinking about Jeremy.

I step away from Del and say, "I have so many questions about what happened to Jeremy. I have to find the answers."

"Let's get off our feet," Del says, "and you can tell me what's on your mind."

So I do. I tell him everything from the beginning. Then I hand him the scrap of paper with the address on it.

"That's a strange place," Del says, "unless Jeremy was going to visit someone over there."

"Why is it strange?"

"Remember the neighborhood?" I shake my head, and he adds, "I took you around there last week. It's where some of those big old homes are."

"Do you think someone Jeremy met might live in one of those houses?"

"Not someone his age. Mostly old folks in those homes." He hands the paper back to me.

"Will you take me over there?"

"Sure, if you want."

"It's as good a starting place as anywhere else. I just wish there was some way to find that car."

He thinks a minute. "Would that satisfy you?"

"What do you mean, satisfy me? I want to

know whose car hit Jeremy."

Again he pauses and seems to study me. Finally he says, "No big deal in finding the car."

I'm surprised at his answer. "But the policeman didn't seem to think the scrap of paint would help, even if they were able to find the car it came from."

"Hey, Angie, wait up," he says. "Don't go getting so upset until you find out what I've got to say. There are four body shops in Fairlie, and my cousin, R.B., works in one of them. If a light blue car's in for repairs, we can probably find out."

"Body shops aren't open on Saturdays."

"My cousin's shop is."

"If the car's not in his shop, how will he find out?"

"He'll know how." Del shakes his head and pulls me out of my chair. "Don't argue, Angie. We'll find out. I promise. And then you can get this off your mind."

I don't understand what Del means by getting it off my mind. As far as I'm concerned, it's a starting place, not an ending. And it's not a promise to count on. Maybe I'm feeling too cynical. But when Del drives me through a back alley, over an oil-stained driveway, to a corrugated-metal building with one side wide open, I begin to believe, and it's hard to breathe, I'm so shaky.

He holds my hand, and we enter the shop. Naturally, I search for a light blue car, but the two dark sedans in the shop don't fit the description.

Del introduces me to a large-boned, grease-stained man whose skin is the burnt color of red earth. He pulls off his gimmie cap and rubs the back of one hand across his forehead, scattering droplets of sweat and leaving streaks of grime.

"Heard about you from Del last week," R.B. says to me. He nods his head in approval.

Del tells him about Jeremy and our search for the

hit-and-run car. I listen and wait for what he'll say.

"Sure sorry about your brother," he says, and I know he means it.

"Can you find the car for us?" It's hard to talk.

"Can't say that. I can ask around, and if there's a blue car in for repairs, I can learn that much. If it's the car you want, that remains to be seen." He looks at me carefully. "If I do find out anything, y'all'uv got to keep me out of it."

"Of course," I tell him. "When can you do this?"

He nudges the tire of the car next to us, rubbing the worn toe of his shoe up and down the tread. Finally he says, "Guess I'd be in a hurry too, girl, if that was my brother that done got hit. Y'all find a place to sit, and get yourselves a Coke or somethin' from the machine, and I'll be back directly."

"Thank you!"

"Wait and see if there's any thanks needed."

"I'm going to take Angie to the place where the accident happened," Del tells him. "We'll be back in just a few minutes."

"Okay," R.B. says. He works his way to a door in a cubicle at one end of the shop.

"Ready?" Del asks, and in a few seconds we're back in his pickup, heading toward the other side of town.

There's not much to talk about. We drive through an elm tunnel to the corner of Avenue G and Huckleberry. He gentles the car to the curb and stops, motor still running.

I don't know what to look at, or look for. My gaze sweeps the streets as they intersect, moving over the curbs and grass. There's a dead end sign on Huckleberry. Down the street a man slowly shovels dirt into a rusty wheelbarrow. But there's no broken glass on the street, no skid marks, nothing to show the horror that took place here just a few hours ago.

I glance down Huckleberry, and suddenly sit a little straighter as a thought whacks me like a slap.

"What's the matter?" Del asks.

"Down this street — at the dead end — isn't that where you showed me the house with the ghost lights?"

"Yep." He looks toward the house. "What does that have to do with Jeremy?"

"I don't know." For some strange reason I can feel the pull of that ugly house with its broken windows and scraggly yard. It's as though the tentacles of its overgrown vines are creeping outward, wiggling toward us.

"I don't think Jeremy would have been there," Del says, his voice so solid and matter-of-fact that it brings me back to reality. "Nobody goes there."

Stumbling through my mind for ideas, I ask, "What if he took a dare?" It makes sense, so I stammer, "What if someone dared Jeremy to go to the haunted house at night?"

Del shakes his head. "Kids were doing that a few years ago, but the neighbors made so much noise about it that the police put a stop to it. Nobody bothers with that old house anymore."

"You said we might investigate it some time!"

His smile is lopsidedly guilty. "I know," he says, "but before we got there I would have thought of something better to do."

"Del!" Maybe I've spent enough energy being angry. I find myself laughing instead.

"Time to get back to R.B.'s," he says, and does a wide U-turn around the street.

It seems to take no time at all to get to the body shop. R.B. is working on one of the cars, and he hunches his way out from under as we approach. "Feller I know works for a dealer, and he knows another feller who works there but does some work

50

on the side, if you know what I mean," he says.

I nod, and R.B. continues. "Light blue car came in last night. Left fender dented, left headlight smashed, bumper shot to hell."

"That might be it!" I find myself shouting, so I do my best to calm down. "Where do we find this car?"

"You ain't gonna find it, girl. That's how come the feller was paid plenty to fix it. That car's already taken care of."

For a moment I close my eyes. "Then we can't find who owns it."

"Sure we can," R.B. says. "Weren't no secret to my friend who's got a little car like that. Grandy Hughes."

The words come in and out of focus. "Grandy Hughes?" The name doesn't mean a thing to me.

Del studies me for a moment, and I can't translate the strange look in his eyes. "Grandy Hughes," he says quietly, "is Debbie's father."

CHAPTER FIVE

All I can do is stare at Del. He stands with his hands at his sides, frowning into space, not saying a word. R.B. shifts from one leg to the other and clears his throat loudly, so I shake myself back to reality and try to thank him for getting the information.

"Del, let's go and see Debbie," I tell him, but he ignores me and talks to R.B. about being a good old boy and seeing him at "Aunt Lou's" on Sunday for dinner.

He takes my hand and tugs me outside to his pickup, which shimmers like a mirage in the afternoon heat. We climb inside, steadying ourselves against the rush of hot air that blasts us before the air conditioner begins to do what it's supposed to do. I ask again. "Can we talk to Debbie now?"

"It won't do any good," he says.

"Why not?"

"If that was her daddy who went to a deal of trouble to cover up, do you think she's going to admit she was driving the car?"

"But the proof—"

"What proof?"

"The sliver of light blue paint, for instance."

"There's lots of light blue cars."

We turn down a residential street. The bright sunlight and dark shadows from the overhead elm branches rapidly flicker against the windshield, making my eyes water.

"If your cousin could find out, so could the police."

"You don't know how small towns work, do you?"

"No! I don't!" I turn to stare at Del. "Why should a small town be different from any place else? People are the same everywhere, aren't they?"

"Nope."

I fling myself back against the seat, anger making my throat hot and tight. "Look, it ought to be simple. The mechanic who told R.B. about Debbie's car could tell the police, couldn't he?"

"But he wouldn't. R.B.'s another good old boy, but the police are somethin' else."

"And everybody around here says *police*! That's not the way it's supposed to be. It's po*leece*!" My fingernails have dug into my hands, so I rub them.

"It's different hereabouts in lots of ways from what you're used to," Del replies so calmly that I feel a shiver of guilt for insulting him. "That's what I'm trying to tell you, Angie. You oil people aren't used to our ways. You'll find the police will be more comfortable believing Debbie's father, 'cause he's grown up with them, gone away to school and then come home to them. He takes care of their banking and loans, and he's big in their church."

"Are you telling me that they'd protect him if he's committed a crime?"

"No. I'm just saying that, the evidence being what it is, they'd believe him before they'd ever believe you." He pauses. "Maybe the police will get on this one. You found out what you wanted, Angie, so why not just stand back and see what happens?"

I notice that we've stopped, and are parked in front of our house. It takes me a few moments to get all the pieces back into place, and Del says, "Angie, about tonight. I know you won't feel like going dancing, so we could do something else. Anything you'd like."

"Del, you were good to help me this afternoon. I owe a lot to you."

"You don't owe me anything."

"You've given me a lot to think about. I — I'd rather just go to the hospital tonight by myself. Okay?"

"Sure," he says. "But if you want me to, I'll go with you. Just call."

Before he can get out of the pickup I open the door and jump down. "Right now I'm not much fun to be with. Why do you want to go with me?"

His words are as direct as his gaze. "I asked myself that same thing," he says. "And I don't have a real good answer. There's just something about you that makes me want to get to know you a lot better."

I'm startled, so I actually blush and stammer, "I'll see you, Del." It's an empty saying, and I trudge into the house wishing I had asked him to stay, yet knowing that it's best for me to be alone for a little while.

Dad greets me with "Where have you been, Angie? We've been concerned about you!"

"With Del," I say quickly. "Tell me about Jeremy. What did the neurologist say?"

"I thought you'd be waiting here to find out."

Mom comes up beside him and says, "Greg, will you just please tell her!"

Mom's smile doesn't match the vague look in her eyes, so I know she's had a few drinks. She rests a hand on Dad's shoulder to balance herself and says, "Dr. Branning thinks that Jeremy's got a good chance."

"Just a chance?"

"There's no way of being sure in a case like Jeremy's," Dad says. "Not at first, that is."

"Not until he's conscious," Mom adds, slurring the last syllable into a hiss.

"I'd like to see him now. Will they let me?"

"Don't you want something to eat first?" Mom

asks. "I was thinking of making dinner soon."

It's strange to think about being hungry at a time like this, but I realize that I am. I'd forgotten about lunch. And I need to tell my parents what I found out with Del.

"I guess so," I say. "But I'll make dinner."

"You're a good girl, Angie," Mom says. Her hug is scented with the wet vegetable smell of her expensive nonallergenic cosmetics, her perfumed body lotion, and fifteen-year-old Scotch.

Later, after I've served dinner, we pick and push at the food on our plates. It's a chore to chew and swallow. I stare at my food, feeling the same frustration a termite must feel in a redwood forest. Finally I give up, put down my fork, lean my elbow on the table without either of my parents reminding me not to, and tell them about Debbie Hughes's car.

I finish by saying "I think we should talk to Debbie and her father."

"No," Dad says. "We'll do this properly. We'll inform the police about what you've learned."

I think about R.B. and his broad, friendly face. "Remember that we'll have to keep Del's cousin out of it."

"The police may ask for a source."

"Dad, it's not fair. R.B. could get in trouble with the friend who gave him the information. He was helping me out, and I've got to help him in return."

The food has steadied Mom. Her eyes focus without any trouble as she says, "I agree with Angie, Greg. You've got people who tip you off about things going on in the oil business, and you don't give them away. Doctors keep their mouths shut, and newspaper reporters, and all sorts of people."

"And we have to," I add.

"Well — Del's cousin didn't happen to tell you how

to find the mechanic who repaired the car, I suppose?"

"No, but he said he works for one of the dealers and repairs stuff on the side."

Dad frowns. "That doesn't tell us anything."

"But the police might be able to find out."

"We have to do something," Mom says. She automatically looks at Dad.

"I'll take Angie to the station," he says. "She can tell them as much as she wants to tell."

I smile at Dad. "I'm ready."

But I guess that no one's really ready to step inside a police station. This one turns out to be a cold, alien room with dull, gray-streaked walls, where a few people who've huddled together toss secret, appraising glances at Dad and me as we hurry across the room to an officer behind a desk. Dad tells him that we'd like to speak to the detective assigned to the case. "It's not called a case," the officer says. "Purely hit 'n' run. We get 'em every once in a while. Not as many as you get in the city, though." He goes back down the hallway, shaking his head, muttering about city people from the oil companies ruining the place.

Dad is patiently persistent, but I can see his temper rising. Finally we're led to a small room, where a heavyset man hoists himself to his feet, leans on his desk as though he needs it to support himself, and holds out his right hand to Dad.

"Detective Tom Fergus," he says. "How's the boy doin'?"

"The doctor's hopeful," Dad says.

"Old Doc Crane can handle things if anyone can."

"We've brought in a neurologist." It's the wrong thing to say. The lines tighten around Detective Fergus's eyes.

"Suit yourself," he mumbles, "but Doc Crane's been good enough for us in Fairlie for forty years."

56

"I didn't imply that he wasn't a skilled doctor," Dad says quickly. "It's just that I know Dr. Branning and his excellent reputation."

Detective Fergus lowers himself into his worn leather chair, which creaks each time he moves. He doesn't ask us to sit, but we do anyway, in the two straight-backed chairs facing him. "Now, what have y'all got on your minds?" he asks.

"My daughter has something to tell you," Dad says. He looks at me, and I stutter like a reject from speech class. Trying to choose my words carefully, I tell him what I learned this morning.

He twists his mouth from side to side as though he's chewing, and after I finish he holds a pursed-lip pose while he stares at me from under his bushy eyebrows. I can't help squirming in my chair.

Finally he says, "Sure would like to know where you got that story, girl."

"My name is Angie."

"Sure. Angie, then."

"Why do you call it a 'story'?"

"Because it don't add up."

I think of what Del tried to tell me, and I still can't believe it. "I want to know why not."

"Don't get riled, girl," he says. He spreads his huge, fat hands out on the desk before him and leans toward me. "Grandy Hughes reported his car stolen Friday night. Then he calls back and says a friend saw it up against a telephone pole, and got on the horn right away to let him know about it. So Grandy got a mechanic he knows to go pick it up and paid him a little extra to get a few dents out, so Debbie could have it to go to school in Monday, and that was that. No secret. No big deal. No cover-up."

Before I can say a word Dad gives a long sigh of relief. "Frankly, I'm very glad to hear the real

57

situation. Thank you for your time, Mr. Fergus."

Dad's halfway out of his chair when I say "But what time was the car supposed to be stolen? Did he report it before or after Jeremy's accident?"

"Don't know what you're gettin' at, but I don't think it matters," the detective tells me. "Simple fact is, it's some other car that done the hit and run."

"How can you be so sure about that? You're not investigating! You're just taking Mr. Hughes's word for what happened!"

His voice is as slow and calm as it was when we came into his office. "Grandy's word is good in this town, girl. I don't find reason to question it."

Dad is on his feet, tugging me to mine. His grip is so firm that my arm aches. "Thank you, again, Mr. Fergus," he says.

When the detective lumbers to his feet he stares at Dad, not me. "Things may be done different in Fairlie than what you oil people are used to wherever y'all come from, but we do them right."

Dad nods quickly, and I find myself half dragged, half pushed out the door, through the main room of the station, and down the steps.

I yank myself out of his grasp as we reach the sidewalk. "I don't believe that man!"

"Don't make unnecessary waves, Angie," Dad says. His voice is tired. "The Hugheses have a logical explanation for what happened to their car and why it was fixed so quickly."

"No one checked into their excuse."

"It wasn't an excuse. It was an explanation. You can't try to do the work the police are supposed to do."

The sun is going down in another red and gold explosion across the wide, pale sky. My father's face is swimming in my sunset-colored tears. I rub them away and see that there are tears in his eyes too. His shoulders sag.

"We can't keep going through this. Just let it alone, Angie," he says. "There is one very important thing you haven't learned. When you move into a new community, you adapt to the people who live there. You don't expect them to adapt to you."

I don't want to get into another long discussion with Dad. I touch his hand. "Will you take me to the hospital? I want to see Jeremy."

We arrive during visiting hours, and the hospital corridors are buzzing. We edge through chatterers and hum-hummers down a long corridor. I begin to turn toward the intensive care section, but Dad grabs my arm and steers me farther down the hall.

"They've put him into a private room," he says.

Carefully, as though we're intruding, we open the door and step inside. An elderly woman in a nurse's uniform pulls herself from the straight-backed chair by Jeremy's bed and smiles at Dad. A wad of bright yellow knitting is clutched in her right hand, and she stuffs it into a large pocket.

"He's doing nicely." The words squeeze through her smile.

She and Dad stand near the door, whispering as though Jeremy will awake if they raise their voices. I leave them and sit in the chair by Jeremy's bed.

He looks so young and vulnerable. I feel a jolt of guilt, remembering the arguments we've had. I wish I could take back all the things I've ever said to hurt him.

Once again I hold my brother's hand. He may not feel it, but it helps me. I study his face, trying to ignore the bandages and bruises.

"I wish you could tell me what happened to you," I whisper. "I don't believe the excuse the police gave me." Jeremy sleeps on. "If there were just some clue, something to tell me where you were Friday night."

I think of his room. I haven't been in it. Our bedrooms have always been our private sanctuaries. I've respected that. Or has the real truth been that I haven't been interested enough in Jeremy to invade his room?

"Do you still have model planes hanging from the ceiling? You used to. How many years ago was that? And I seem to remember a terrarium. You were raising tadpoles into frogs. Oh, Jeremy, that was when you were nine years old! What are you interested in now? And where have I been that I haven't cared to notice?"

The pressure of Dad's hand on my shoulder startles me, and I jump. "We'd better go," he murmurs.

"Where?"

"Why, home, of course."

"We haven't been here very long. There are things I want to tell Jeremy."

"He can't hear you, Angie."

"We don't know that."

He sighs. "Please be reasonable."

I lean toward my brother. "Good night, Jeremy. I'll be back tomorrow." There are tiny blue veins on his eyelids. His lashes lie quietly on his cheeks. I wish I could reach behind that curtain. "Good night."

It's not late when we reach our house, but Mom has gone to sleep facedown on the sofa in the den, her cheek squashed against her nose so that her breathing comes out in a whispery snuffle.

Dad looks down on her for a few moments, his mouth drooping like an unhappy little boy's.

He needs someone. "You want to talk about Jeremy, Dad?" I ask him.

But he shakes his head. "I'd better get a light blanket for your mother," he answers. "I don't want her to catch cold."

I wait until he returns and tucks an old, blue, woven shawl around her. "I couldn't find the blankets." His voice seems to belong to someone else.

"Dad, it might help us both to talk about Jeremy. Maybe about what we can do for him."

"Everything that can be done is being done, Angie." He straightens both inside and outside. "Dr. Branning knows what to do." He moves toward the rosewood desk in the corner. "Now, if you'll excuse me, I've got some paperwork to do."

"Do you have to do it now?"

"Yes, now." His look is almost conciliatory. "Besides, we don't want to wake your mother, do we?"

I wander off to my room, see that it's only eight thirty, and wonder what to do with myself. I pick up my French book, but toss it on to my desk with a groan. Not now. There is no way to forget the accident, the detective, and Debbie Hughes.

Suddenly I find myself picking up my handbag and car keys. I've got to talk to Debbie. It won't take long. I should be home again before Dad goes to bed and looks for me to say good night. The Grandy Hughes address is in the phone book, and by this time I'm familiar with the streets.

There's a car in the Hughes driveway and some lights on in the downstairs rooms. A far upper-left window also gleams in the darkness. It dawns on me that Debbie probably isn't here. She's bound to have a date on Saturday night. But I've come this far. I'll give it a try.

The doorbell's chimes are followed by the click of a woman's heels. The door opens, and a short woman with blond hair in a high, teased, out-of-style hairdo smiles at me. "Yes, dear?"

"My name is Angie." I deliberately leave off my

last name. "I'd like to see Debbie, if she's home."

"My, yes, she's home, all right," the woman says. "But you can't see her. She has some little virus or something, and you know how catching those things can be."

"I won't worry about that," I tell her. "It's very important to me to see Debbie."

Her eyelids stretch wide and blink. "But she may not feel up to seeing anyone, dear. She's broken a date to stay in bed, so she probably won't want to talk to you."

"Please. Could you ask her?"

"Well—" she looks over her shoulder, then shrugs. "All right. You said your name is Angie?"

I nod.

"Wait just a minute, Angie." The door closes gently in my face.

A breeze has come up again. It must be a regular thing around here. At least it's a layer of cool to break up the pounding heat. But the breeze carries a grit of dust in it, which crawls down my neck, sifting into my clothes.

It's at least five minutes before the woman returns. I assume she's Debbie's mother. I also assume she and Debbie have had some kind of conversation about me, because she has gulped down her smile and she opens the door just a crack. Her eyes are narrowed and wary.

"Debbie doesn't feel well enough to see anyone, just as I told you."

"Please, Mrs. Hughes. I must see her."

"No, no. Not now."

The door begins to shut, but I move a little closer and say, "Listen to me, Mrs. Hughes. If I can't talk to Debbie now, I'll come back tomorrow, and the day after that, and the day after that, if necessary. Or I'll talk about what's on my mind in school. Yes. That's what I'll do."

"What a rude young woman you are," she says, but her voice wavers. "If Grandy were just here, he could—"

I don't find out what Grandy Hughes could do, because a voice behind Mrs. Hughes says, "It's all right, Mama. Let her come in."

"Oh, dear," her mother says, but she opens the door, and I quickly step inside.

Debbie's wearing a pink shortie nightgown, and her feet are bare. Her hair is tousled, and she looks like someone who needs to be in bed. For the first time I have some doubts about what I've started.

The Hughes home is beautiful, with a wide, circular staircase sweeping up from the entry hall, but there's a fussy, busy accumulation of too many pictures and too many accent pieces. There are even too many people here right now. I want to talk to Debbie, not to her mother.

"I'm sorry if you're sick," I tell her. "If you'd like to get back in bed, I'll be glad to talk to you in your room. What I want to ask you won't take long."

"Okay," she says, looking at her mother instead of me. "Mama, you don't need to come with us. We don't have much to say to each other. Angie will be leaving in a few minutes."

As I follow Debbie up the stairs, her mother scuttles into another room. "You'd do it, too, wouldn't you?" Debbie's words are flat and angry, taking me off guard.

"Do what?"

"Hassle me at school. I heard what you said to Mama."

"I don't want to hassle you. What makes you think I'd try to do a thing like that?"

At the top of the staircase Debbie doesn't pause.

She just heads down the hall and into a room to the left. It's the one I had seen from the street.

Debbie flops on her bed, leaning against the padded, pastel-flowered headboard. "Tom Fergus called Daddy about your trip to the police station. He told him what you said."

I stand by the door, watching her. "And he told us your excuse — your explanation," I say.

"Then what are you doing here?"

"Trying to find out the truth."

"What Daddy told him is the truth."

"You really want me to believe that after your car was stolen your father would rush like that to get the body work done on it?"

"I need my car to get back and forth to school."

"One of your friends could have picked you up."

"I don't want to be dependent on my friends."

I take two steps closer to Debbie, and she flattens against the headboard. "Don't lie to me. I believe that you were in that car, that you hit my brother."

"No," she says. "I'm going to tell you where I was, and you aren't going to like it. Not a little bit. But the way you're acting, you deserve it."

She sits upright, and her eyes glitter as she smiles. "Last night," she says, "I was out with your friend Del Scully."

CHAPTER SIX

I hope she can't see how she's shaken me. "I don't believe you."

"Why not?"

"Because Del's not in your social group. He's—"

She interrupts with a slow laugh that rolls huskily from deep in her throat. "Sometimes that doesn't matter. He's *very* good-looking. Don't you agree?"

I hate myself for blushing. I try to act as calmly as possible, because I realize that I've let her get me off the track. "Someone phoned me," I say. "Was it you?"

She drops the pose. "What are you talking about?"

"About a phone call I got from a coward who whispered 'Your brother is dead' and hung up."

I watch her carefully, but I can't tell if what I said surprised her or she's just reacting to hearing me say the words. There's a quick intake of breath and her eyes widen. "Why do you think I'd make a phone call like that?"

"Because I think it was your car that hit my brother."

"My car was stolen."

"Prove it."

"I don't have to prove anything to you." She's leaning forward, and her shoulders are trembling.

I step a little closer to her. I'm shaking, too, but it's because I'm so angry. "Maybe you were driving your car, maybe not. If you weren't, then I think you know who was, and that makes you equally guilty. My brother is still unconscious. He's badly hurt. And I'm not going to let the hit-and-run driver get away. If that creep is also the whisperer, then there's even more to answer for."

"Get out of here!" Her voice is so tight the words seem to scratch her throat.

"Okay — for now. But I won't give up."

"Leave me alone!"

I don't answer. I just give her one long stare before I turn and walk out of her bedroom. Her mother is standing at the bottom of the stairs like a watchdog who's ready to go for the throat. I wonder how much of our conversation she's overheard. There's nothing to say to her, so I just pass her and walk across the entrance hall to the front door. She's right behind me, and I hear the dead bolt click as the door shuts almost against my back.

She has turned off the porch light, so I stand without moving for a few moments, waiting to get my bearings.

My car isn't the only one on the street, but I'm not aware of that until I'm inside my car and pulling away from the curb. Then I realize that another car started up when mine did. Could it be a coincidence?

I'm not sure, so I circle the block. So does the other car. I pick up speed. The best place for me to be is on one of the main streets, not a residential street. It's hard to breathe and my hands are clammy. I keep glancing from the street to my rearview mirror and back again.

A cross street that can be counted on to have the Fairlie version of traffic is just half a block ahead when a cherry suddenly flashes on top of the car that's following me, and it quickly slides up beside me.

I move to the edge of the curb, and the police car

pulls just in front of me, blocking my way forward. A tall, lanky offer climbs out of the car and walks back toward mine, so I roll down the window. In the glare of red flashes and bounced-off light from my headlights against his car, I recognize him as the same policeman who questioned me in the hospital.

"Hi," I say, and I lean back against the seat feeling weak with relief. "Thank goodness it's you. When I saw I was being followed it scared me."

He looks uncomfortable. "Got your driver's license handy? I need to see it," he says. "Your proof-of-insurance card too."

"Sure." I fumble in my handbag for my wallet, pull out my license and the card and hand them to him. "What's the matter?"

"Routine," he says. He studies the license.

"Why were you following me? What's going on?"

He hands back my license and my insurance card and leans his arms on the frame of my open door window, arching his neck and bending awkwardly like a long-necked crane so that his face is down on a level with mine. "Look," he says. "A few years ago my brother-in-law was in a bad smash-up. Drunk driver caused it. The drunk walked away from it, but my brother-in-law died and left my sister a widow with two little kids to support. I hated that drunk so bad I could have killed him. Almost did."

He pauses, and I say, "I'm sorry. But I don't understand what's happening now. Here and right now."

"I'm trying to say I know how you feel about what all went down with your brother. But what you're doin', runnin' around hassling people, won't help any."

"I wasn't hassling anybody."

"Miz Hughes felt different. She put in a call. You're probably a good kid who's a lot upset. It's just that you make a pest of yourself and you're gonna get watched."

67

I understand what he's trying to tell me. My body feels numb from the shock, and I wiggle my fingers as though they've gone to sleep. "Nothing is going to get done," I'm mumbling to myself, but he picks up the words.

"Hit 'n' runs are hard to prove."

I put my hands on the steering wheel, gripping it tightly. "I get the picture. Can I go home now?"

"Sure," he says. He straightens, hunching his shoulders up and down and stretching to get out the kinks. "I'll just follow along to make sure you get home all right."

He moves back to his car with long, slow strides and climbs in, flipping off the red cherry. He moves forward to give me space, waiting for me to take off.

I've got to think. There's so much to think about. I try to pretend he's not there, and as I pull up on the driveway I ignore him.

Dad has heard the back door open and close. He comes into the kitchen, a pencil in his hand, his shirtsleeves rolled up. His reading glasses have slid crookedly on his nose, and he takes them off, blinking at me like a surprised owl. "I thought you were in bed, Angie."

"I just went out for a few minutes."

"You should have told me."

"You were busy. I didn't want to bother you."

Fear suddenly shivers across his face and is gone before I can be sure that I've seen it. He reaches to hug me, holding me against his shoulder and saying, "Angie, we *must* know where you are — especially after dark. We don't want anything else —" He can't finish the sentence.

I suddenly feel protective toward my father and hug him back, awkwardly patting his shoulder. "Okay, Dad. I didn't think. I'm sorry."

He straightens, holding me off and giving me a little shake and a smile. "Fine," he says, and he's back to the father I know. "It's time we headed for bed. Your mother has been asleep for hours."

I think of Del, and in the confusion of my feelings I blurt out, "Did anyone call me?"

"No," Dad says. "Of course not, or I would have known you weren't here."

To cover up I reach for a glass and get a drink of water.

"Were you expecting a call?" Dad asks.

"No," I answer, gulping down the lukewarm water and wiping my mouth on the back of my arm.

Who cares about you, Del? I'm astounded at the jealousy I feel, the hurt because I was beginning to trust him. I try to be rational. There's been nothing between Del and me. Nothing to give me a reason for aching like this. I slap at my hair with a hairbrush and viciously scrub my teeth. I squirm between the sheets, tugging at my twisting pajamas, and lie there in the dark. *Del*, I think, *why didn't you tell me you were out with Debbie?*

Sleep is an eraser. It's like one of those magic tablets I had when I was a kid, with the black stuff under a heavy sheet of plastic. I could write on the plastic and the words would show, then zip! Pull it up and everything I'd written had disappeared. It was only later, when I'd look closely at the black part, that I could see the imprint of the words still imbedded there.

In the morning I come out of a dream where I'm with Meredith. The black stuff with the deeply cut words shows up, and I remember.

I swing my feet over the edge of the bed. I want to go to the hospital right away to see Jeremy. I have a plan.

69

Mom and Dad are still asleep, so I dress as quietly as I can and — remembering my promise to Dad — leave a note against the salt shaker on the kitchen table as I swallow a slice of bread and a small glass of milk.

In just a few minutes I'm at the hospital, walking into Jeremy's room. Another woman sits by his bed. Same gray hair, same encouraging smile, even the same knitting — only pink, instead of yellow.

I introduce myself, and she says, "He rested well all night." She glances around the room. "I'll get another chair."

"I'll be right here," I say, "if you want to go to the ladies' room or get something to eat or go outside for a smoke."

That was the magic button. "Well," she says, "as long as someone's with him. That's what your father wants."

She leaves, and I hitch the chair a little closer to the bed. Again I take Jeremy's hand and stroke the back of it. For a few moments we sit there silently.

Finally, I say, "I couldn't wait to get here to talk to you, Jeremy, and now I don't know what to talk about!"

Naturally he doesn't answer. I knew he wouldn't, even though I waited as if he would. "I mean I've read about some people who've talked to people in their families who were unconscious, and sometimes it's helped to bring them back. I'm going to do that with you, but I honestly don't know what you're interested in. You're my brother, and I don't know anything about you. Should I talk to you about your friends? I guess I don't know any of your friends, except Boyd. You play tennis, and I don't know anything about the school tennis team. And none of us knows where you were Friday night."

His hand moves slightly in mine, and I lean forward,

70

holding my breath. "Jeremy? Can you hear me?"

But Jeremy sleeps.

"Listen, Jeremy," I try again. "I wouldn't like it if anyone went through the stuff in my room — especially my brother. So I hope you're not going to get mad at me or anything, but I'm going to check out the things in your desk. Please don't mind too much, Jeremy."

I stroke his hand again. "All this time I thought of you as only somebody living in the same house, and I never thought about what you needed or thought of or wanted. Does that make any sense?"

"It does to me."

The voice comes from right behind me, and I jump straight out of the chair. "Mom! You scared me!"

There are tears in her eyes, and she says, "Angie, I didn't mean to listen in. But you were so wrapped up in what you were saying to Jeremy that I couldn't interrupt you."

"It's okay." I pull the chair toward her. "Come on. Sit down."

"No, that's your chair."

"Mom, sit down. I'll get another chair."

I walk into the empty room across the hall, wishing that this place didn't smell so strongly of pine-scented cleanser. Pines should be woods and glens and damp places with rotted bark and curling ferns — not hospital floors. It's a terrible way to cheat. I pick up a chair and carry it back, placing it on the other side of Jeremy's bed.

Neither of us says anything for a while. The room is quiet enough for me to hear the tiny rhythmic drips of the I.V. feeding Jeremy's arm. Mom's perfume floats over to me, adding a comforting softness to the room.

I want Mom to understand what I'm doing, so I tell her. "I believe that Jeremy can hear us. I think if we

71

talk to him we can reach through and pull him back."

"Do you?" She's hopeful as she glances back at Jeremy. "What should we say to him, Angie? Should we tell him how much we love him?"

She looks as lost as I feel, so I reach across the bed and put a hand on her shoulder. "Why don't you tell him about the tennis matches on national TV?"

She blinks at me. "I don't even know who's playing."

"Well," I say, "I know a couple of them, but I have no idea about the scores."

Mom starts getting fidgety. She squirms in her chair and brushes invisible crumbs off the blanket and throws little side glances at Jeremy as though she's not sure she's ever seen him before. When she looks at her watch the second time I say, "It's too early for a drink."

I guess it came out harder than I'd meant it to, because she looks hurt and says, "I wasn't thinking of having a drink, Angie. You act as though I'm an alcoholic."

I mumble, "I'm sorry. It's just that you do seem to drink a lot."

There's a long pause, and she says, "Sometimes it helps."

"You said that before, Mom. I don't know what it helps."

She looks at me with eyes so much the dark blue color of my own; yet I feel she's talking not to me but to herself. "Each place we go, I start over," she says. "I join clubs and smile at strangers. I belong to study groups and study things I haven't the vaguest interest in. Or is it 'in which I haven't the vaguest'? Oh, well. I go to dinner parties and luncheons given by people who've asked me just because my husband's job is more important than their husbands' jobs."

"Listen, Mom, I didn't mean to—"

"You complain about missing friends each time we've been transferred. Don't you think it's the same with me? I learned a long time ago to put up barriers, to never allow myself to cry over a friend I might never see again."

I feel so weird hearing all this from my mother. I don't know what to answer. I don't know if she even expects an answer. Awkwardly I pat the hand she has resting on the bed and stumble to my feet. "I'd better get back to the house. I never did get my French assignment finished."

She just gives me a vacant smile as though she's traveled somewhere I'm not allowed and says, "I'll stay with Jeremy a while, Angie. Your father will probably be here soon too."

"Want me to start something for dinner?"

"We can go somewhere later. I don't know. There must be a restaurant nearby."

We stare at each other, and she adds, "Well, there's always the club."

I stoop to kiss the top of her head and pause, looking at Jeremy. I have got to reach through to him. And I've got to find out what happened. It's a strange feeling, as though if I don't find out, Jeremy won't ever come back. "Good-bye, Jeremy," I murmur. "I'll see you later."

I think I see his arm move, just slightly. Mom doesn't react, so maybe it's just my imagination.

My feelings about Jeremy are so strong that when I come into the empty house I make straight for his room, stopping at the doorway because I feel like an intruder. Papers and books are mounded on his desk, and the dark red-plaid spread on his bed is pulled askew over lumps and bumps in the blanket. I step over his tennis shoes as I walk to his desk, and pick up a few papers that have slipped to the floor.

I pull out the chair that's tucked into the kneehole in Jeremy's desk and sit in it. I divide the books and papers into two sections: books neatly to the left, papers to the right. I glance through the papers. School assignments. A bookmark hangs from one of the books. Jeremy's reading *Captain Horatio Hornblower*? I wonder if it's an assignment or if it's a story he's really into.

I slide open the center top drawer. It's a jumble of broken pencils, gum wrappers, even an old yo-yo. But there's a slender book on top of the mess. It's the size of a ledger, with a deep brown cover. I reach for it as though I've been told to do so, and as I open the cover I hold my breath.

Poetry by J. D. Dupree.

Jeremy writes poetry?

I turn the page gingerly, terrified at stumbling into Jeremy's secrets.

I soon forget that I'm an intruder. The first few poems wouldn't even be a threat to Rod McKuen; but the literary quality doesn't matter. It's Jeremy's thoughts that are on these pages, and I'm discovering a brother I hadn't known existed. He writes of loneliness, of the terrors of moving to new places. He writes of feelings I can share, and I'm ashamed that I thought those feelings were mine alone. But there's a hopelessness in some of the poems that frightens me. I read one of them aloud, and the words hang shivering long after I've spoken them:

> *I grab at stars,*
> *sweeping my hand across the heavens,*
> *hanging onto sharp chunks of hope*
> *that cut my palm.*
> *Carefully, eagerly I pry open*
> *my fingers*

and find I have captured
only slivers of darkness.

Some of the pages in the book have been torn out.
I read through a couple more poems before I come to
the last one. Beyond this page lie clean, blank pages
that are ready for his thoughts to come.

As I read this poem I begin to tremble. The hand-
writing is a hasty scrawl of black ink, and the first
line has been scratched out and written over. It's a
strange poem, different from the others, but it's here
for a reason, and I feel it tugging at me:

The house is haunted
by the Ghosts of Now
whose shadows no one wants to see,
whose screams no one wants to hear,
until tomorrow.

What are you saying Jeremy? I don't understand.
I'm staring at the page, but it's as though I've closed
my eyes and have dreamed up a picture. In front of
me is the haunted house that Del pointed out. It's
rotting under those twisting, unkempt vines, its
windows blank eyes that shut off the ghostly world
inside its walls. It's a real house, not an allegory.
Jeremy told me to stay away from that house. Why?

I close the book, replacing it in the drawer,
shutting it carefully away. Now I know what my next
step is. I've got to find those "ghosts of now" and
discover what they know about my brother.

CHAPTER SEVEN

The Andrews place squats alone at the end of an empty, quiet street. Maybe it's because of the over-large lot that surrounds it; maybe it's because the house looks like an unkempt, yellowed old man who badly needs a barber, but I feel that the other houses on the block have cringed away from this place, tucking in their tidy porches and neat walkways and dropping filmy curtains over blank eyes.

I park in front of the house and pick my way up the cracked cement walk. The air glitters with sunlit dust that stirs from gray-coated leaves and grass and sifts back into place as I pass. A large oak near the front porch has died, its withered branches wound mummy-like by a strangling vine that creeps from the tree to the dry, curling shingles on the roof of the house. One of the wooden pillars on the front porch has cracked and bent, allowing the roof to sag over the entrance way, but the dark front door stands strong and forbidding.

Someone once lived in this house and loved it, and for a few moments I feel sad that it should be so neglected, left alone to die.

But the house is not dead.

There are small rustlings, creakings, and sounds barely loud enough to be heard as the house moves and breathes with the midday heat. I feel that it's watching me, waiting to see what I'll do. Or could someone be watching? Someone be listening, just as I listen?

Quickly I shake my head, trying to toss away scraps of fear, and climb the shaky steps to the front porch.

The windows are draped with some fabric that closes off the view inside. There are cracks here and there where the drapes don't quite meet or the fabric has split, but the places are narrow and too high up for me to see through. I move from one end of the porch to the other, trying to peer inside. I shove at the front door, which grunts and holds fast. My scruffy footprints have disturbed the dust of the porch, and I feel uncomfortable, almost as though I should apologize.

Maybe around the back I'll have better luck. The yard is full of uneven holes and mounds, with scraggly branches of untended bushes laid out like traps to catch ankles. Now and then I look up at the house, and each time I have the clammy feeling that I'm being watched. Not by one of the neighbors. I glance over my shoulder and up and down the street to make sure. No one is outside. There are no movements of curtains at neighbors' windows. The watcher is in this house. I feel it.

It's a big house, with rooms jutting out at the side like afterthoughts; it takes more than a few minutes to walk around to the back. The yard here is only a dried tangle, a graveyard of what was once someone's garden. In back there is a garage that opens onto an alley. Between the side door of the garage and the back entrance of the house is a cracked, buckling cement walk. A narrow stoop of three cement steps leads up to a torn screen door that is hanging crookedly by its bottom hinge. I climb the steps, edge past the door, and find myself in a small service porch where the faded green linoleum on the floor curls away from the walls. There is something wrong about that linoleum. It should have a heavy layer of dust, as the front porch had, and it doesn't. People have walked across this floor — and more than once.

I can hear my own heart pounding. My breathing is loud, and I wonder if the house is listening to me. Why am I so afraid?

Before I can reason with myself I grab for the doorknob, but it refuses to turn. Even the knob of a locked door would turn, wouldn't it? Or is someone on the other side of the door, clutching the knob to keep me from turning it?

Suddenly I let go, and I see the knob jiggle before it settles into place. Yes. Someone is there. Who is it? One of those ghosts whose screams no one wants to hear?

"Angie?"

The voice hits me in the back like a sudden blow. I shriek and whirl toward the voice, grabbing at the air, trying to find something to hang onto.

"Hey!" Del says. He's standing below the cement steps, and he holds up both hands, palms toward me. "I thought you heard me coming. I didn't mean to scare you, Angie. I wouldn't want to do that."

My words straggle through gulps of air. "I didn't hear you. I was listening to — I didn't know you were — What are you doing here, Del?"

"Looking for you," he says. "I saw your car parked on the street."

"But how did you know I'd be here, at this house?"

"I didn't. I thought you might be —" He stops and looks in the direction of the intersection. "You weren't at home. You weren't at the hospital. When I got to the end of the street I saw your car parked down here."

I'm surprised how glad I am to see Del. But the

gladness is mixed with anger as I remember the way Debbie looked when she told me they'd been together Friday evening. Del hadn't told me about being with Debbie. I had begun to trust him, but he hadn't been honest with me.

Del cocks his head and stares at me. "Did you just say you were listening to something? What?"

Whatever is on the other side of that door might be waiting for my answer too. Stiffly I walk across the porch and down the steps and face Del. "Why were you looking for me?"

Del shoves his hat to the back of his head and scratches his forehead. "Seems like we've got a lot of questions without answers." When I don't say anything he adds, "Okay. Me first. I wanted to tell you something."

"About Debbie?"

He looks puzzled. "Nope. Not exactly. I got word about your being stopped by one of the cops. I wanted to tell you that things don't work here the way they probably did in the city where you came from. Don't try to push this, Angie. You'll be the one who gets hurt."

For an instant I close my eyes and take a deep breath. I *am* the one who was hurt. "Then you know I went to see Debbie."

He nods.

"Do you know everything? Do you know what she told me?"

"Don't get so riled." His hands rest on my shoulders. "I don't know what you're getting at, so why don't you just tell me instead of yelling at me?"

"I didn't mean to yell. It's just that — Why didn't you tell me that you were with Debbie Friday night?"

"*With* Debbie? I'd hardly call it that."

"That's what Debbie said."

He chuckles, low in his throat. "Did she tell you about the others on the senior party committee who were there too? We had a meeting to work out stuff for the graduation dance that will come up next semester."

"A meeting? But then afterward—?"

The question hangs there, unfinished. Del shakes his head. "Afterward I went to my aunt's house. Angie, I don't know what Debbie told you, but that's the way it was."

I'm surprised at the relief that rushes through my whole body with a happy, zingy sensation, like bubbles in my bloodstream. "Del, I'm sorry. She was just so convincing, and I was upset. I don't know why she lied to me. She made it sound as though you dated each other."

"We did," he says, "but not Friday night."

All I can think of to say is, "Oh." I hope the jealousy doesn't show.

"Don't press Debbie too hard," Del says. "The most important thing you've got to worry about is your brother gettin' better. Finding out what happened to him doesn't matter that much right now."

"No one can stop me from getting to the truth." I take a long look at Del. "Like that person who did the body work on Debbie's car. I thought maybe you'd help me find him."

Del scuffs the toe of one of his well-worn boots against the bottom step and says, "I'm one ahead of you there, but I found out something you won't like. He left town on what I guess you could call a paid vacation, according to what my cousin said."

"Surely the police could find him."

"Yeah, but I doubt if they'll look for him. There's still no proof that Debbie's car hit your brother."

"That's not fair!"

"Lots of things aren't fair, Angie. But you've got to be realistic. Without real evidence they can't make a case."

I sag against him, and he puts his arms around me. "There's so much I need to find out — so much about Jeremy too."

"You didn't answer the question I asked you," Del says. "You told me you were listening to something. Listening to what?"

"I don't know. I walked around this house and felt as though I were being watched. And when I tried the back door I got the feeling that someone was on the other side, holding it shut."

"It's probably locked tight."

"Maybe. But I want to go in this house. I can't get it out of my mind. This house might be able to tell me something."

"You playing hunches or getting into ESP? I don't understand what this house has got to do with Jeremy."

"Because Jeremy —" I begin to tell Del about Jeremy's poem, but something holds me back, so I say, "I think that Jeremy knew something about this house. He warned me not to come here. I have to know why."

For a few moments Del looks at me. Then his fingers twine through mine, and he leads me up the steps and into the back porch. "We'll go through this old place together. And if we get picked up for breaking and entering it will be your job to post bail, because I'm down to my last ten bucks."

The doorknob turns easily under Del's grip, and I shiver.

"Nothin' to be scared about," Del says. "You were probably tugging it the wrong way."

But I wasn't.

The kitchen's high wooden cabinets and huge gas

stove are out of a museum catalogue. A pair of grimy aluminium salt and pepper shakers sits on the shelf above the burners, and a tea kettle rests on the stove's metal wings. A ragged straw broom leans against the far wall. Even the sunlight coming in the bare window over the large, chipped sink doesn't improve this room.

"This poor old house," I whisper, as though the house can hear us. I stick close to Del.

There's an open door, leading to a dim room that looks like a dining room. But there are two closed doors to our right. I simply point toward them, and Del seems to read my mind.

"Probably open to a broom closet and a storm cellar." He looks down at me. "The early houses around here had cellars where people could go in case of tornadoes."

"Should we go down there?"

"I doubt if we'd find anything more than a stray rattler."

I shudder. "Let's check the other rooms instead."

The fear remains, even with Del at my side. We're picking our way through a skeleton, with someone's memories blowing aside like dust under our footsteps. The cobwebs and faded carpets, the old plush-covered chairs and the photographs on the wall accent the gaps where a few valuable pieces of furniture must have been. The remains of the deceased.

But where are the ghosts?

We have moved through the rooms on the first floor, passing the heavy staircase that leads upward to a landing, then turns.

Del stops and looks at me. "Well?" he asks. "Do you still think someone is here?"

"No." I try a smile. "I guess that ghosts must stay out of sight until after dark." The rooms are chill, even in the midday heat, but whoever had been here has gone.

"Then let's forget about looking upstairs and get out of this place," Del says. "I'll follow you home, and if you haven't got anything better to do, we can get hamburgers."

We leave the house by the front door. It's got one of those locks that automatically fastens without a key.

"Ghosts don't leave footprints," Del says, staring at the front porch.

"Those are my footprints. I was on the porch, trying to look in the windows." I stoop, leaning down to stare at the boards. "I know I wasn't wearing one shoe and one tennis shoe."

"Which means?"

"Look," I say, pointing at a partial ridged footprint in the dust. I stand, and we stare at each other for just a moment. "Someone was in the house. He left by the front door."

"He or she. There's only part of a print. The rest must have been scuffed."

"On purpose."

"We don't know that." Del looks down the street. "Why would anyone be in this house?"

I can't help glancing at the shut-in face of the house. "Maybe it's something we wouldn't notice, something that can't be seen."

"Forget it for now," Del says. "It could also have been some kid in the neighborhood who hides out here for kicks."

We leave it like that.

It's good to forget for a little while. I drop our car at the house, climb into Del's pickup, and spend a couple of hours munching through fat hamburgers and skinny fries and talking about nothing important because just being together is important enough. I memorize the crinkle laugh lines around the outer corners of Del's eyes and the firmness of his lips and the way one corner of his mouth turns up more than the other when he smiles. So he cares for me, does he? Well, maybe I'm beginning to care for him.

Finally he squeezes out of his side of the booth and holds out a hand to me. "Time for me to tend to my chores. Got some horses to get in."

"I'd like to see your horses some time," I say.

"Want to ride?"

"I don't know how."

"I'm a good teacher."

"Then I'd love to — after Jeremy's better." As we walk to the truck I cling to Del's hand and say, "He *will* get better. I've got to help him get better."

"I know," Del murmurs.

As Del parks in front of our walkway, Mom comes around the corner of the house carrying a small birdhouse that's painted yellow with a green roof. She holds it up as we climb out of the pickup and walk toward her. "Hello, Del," she says. "I'm looking for a good place to put Jeremy's birdhouse." She stares at the birdhouse as though she's never seen it before and adds, "Jeremy made this for me when he was a cub scout, years ago. We moved so often, it just didn't seem worthwhile to put it up, and I packed it away."

"How is Jeremy?" Del asks.

"The same. The doctor says that all Jeremy's vital signs are good." She takes a long breath that comes out in a shudder. "But he doesn't wake up. He just keeps sleeping."

"Maybe that's good for him," Del says. "While he's sleeping his body is working to heal itself."

"Yes," Mom says.

Del takes the birdhouse out of her hands. "Y'all tell me where you want this, and I'll hang it for you."

"Where?" Mom repeats. "Oh, I don't know."

"How about that mulberry between your house and garage? It's a sheltered place, and Jeremy could see his birdhouse hanging there when you bring him home."

"That's a great idea," I answer, and Mom's head bobs in agreement.

It takes Del just a few minutes. He returns, accepts Mom's thanks, and we all just stand there. I'm desperately trying to think of something light and conversational to say when Del says, "Is it okay if I get a drink of water?"

"Sure," I say. "I'll get it for you."

"I don't want to bother you," he says. "I know where your kitchen is. You and your mother go take a look at the birdhouse. See if I put it in the right place."

Mom and I walk around the side of the house and stare up at the birdhouse.

"Very nice," Mom says.

"It looks good there," I tell her.

This is dumb, I think. *Why are we here, staring up at a birdhouse?*

Del strides across the lawn, a smile on his face. "Everything okay?"

"Lovely," Mom says, and she thanks him again.

He grins at me. "See you, Angie," he says, and leaves.

As we watch his pickup move down the street Mom says, almost grudgingly, "He does seem like a nice, friendly boy, Angie."

I put an arm around her shoulders and lead her into the house, through the back door into the kitchen. "Where's Dad?"

"He's at the hospital."

"Have you had anything to eat?"

"I don't remember."

I pull out a kitchen chair and guide her into it. "Mom, I'll make you a sandwich. Okay?"

"That's too much."

"All right. I know we've got crackers and cheese. I'll put them on the table, and you can eat as much as you like." While I'm talking I'm moving, and before she can object the food is in front of her along with a plate and a knife.

"Don't you want some cheese too?" Mom asks. I'm glad that she has begun to eat.

"Del and I had hamburgers."

I guess I expect her to ask where I've been, or something about Del, but she's off somewhere, probably with Jeremy.

Mom doesn't need me now, so I go into the den and quickly look up Debbie Hughes's phone number. The anger burns more fiercely when I hear her mother's voice.

Making my own voice light and giggly I say, "Hi, Mrs. Hughes. May I please speak to Debbie?"

"Yes, dear," she says, and I can almost hear her thinking that she obviously should recognize the voice of someone who must be one of Debbie's friends. "Just one minute, and I'll call her."

Debbie picks up the extension in her room. I wait to hear Mrs. Hughes replace her receiver while Debbie says, "Hello? Hello?"

The click comes, and I say, "Why did you lie to me?"

"What?"

"I said, 'Why are you lying?' Debbie, were you the one driving the car that hit my brother?"

"You stop this! You hear? You stop bothering me!"

"I'm not going to stop until I find out what happened to my brother. And if your mother gets the police on my back again, I'm going to work even harder to make sure the hit-and-run driver goes to jail — especially if the driver was you."

"I don't know what you mean about my mother!"

"Why don't you ask her? And ask her and your father where they sent the mechanic who did the cover-up on your car." If Debbie's answers I don't hear it, because I'm so angry my hands are shaking, and I hang up.

I rest my head on my arms for a few moments, taking deep breaths, beating down the anger. Finally I'm okay; so I wander back to Jeremy's room and sit at his desk. I want to read his poetry again.

As soon as the drawer is open I see a gleam of gold, a sliver of metal shining under a wad of paper next to the notebook. I pull out a wristwatch. It's a man's watch, and I know it's expensive without looking at the make. Who's been in the drawer? The watch wasn't here when I first read Jeremy's poetry. I would have noticed it. Wouldn't I?

There are a couple of paperback books on the desk. They're not textbooks. And a tennis team schedule. I don't remember these things being here when I first looked in Jeremy's desk.

Where did this watch come from?

There's a gold band, and on the back of the watch an inscription in tiny block letters: *To Phil with love from Alice.*

I don't understand. Who is Phil? I glance around the room as though the answer should be written on the walls.

But the answer comes like a slam between the shoulder blades. I gasp and shudder as I realize this is probably a stolen watch, and someone has put it in Jeremy's desk drawer. If the watch has been put here, then other things might be hidden here too. So I search.

It's hard to look for something when you don't know what to look for. And I don't know Jeremy's things well enough to recognize them. But any item planted here would be valuable, and I can't find anything that looks as though it wouldn't belong to a fifteen-year-old boy.

Except for the watch.

Who put it here?

I don't want to tell Mom. I don't think she can handle it, and I don't know yet what it means. So I slide the watch into the back hip pocket of my jeans and go to the kitchen, where Mom is still sitting at the table, staring at some crumbs of drying cheese.

"Did anyone come by today?" I ask.

Mom frowns a little as she looks at me. I feel as though she's trying to remember who I am and what I'm doing here, so I repeat the question. "Mom, did anyone come to the house while I was gone?"

"Oh," she says. "Boyd brought a couple of books that he thought Jeremy might like to read." She shakes her head. "I tried to tell him that Jeremy wasn't ready for anything like that, but — well, it was very thoughtful of Boyd, wasn't it?"

"Very," I answer, finding it hard to talk through my anger. "I suppose he put the books on Jeremy's desk."

Mom looks at me sharply. "What's the matter with you, Angie?"

"I'm sorry, Mom. I didn't mean anything. I just wondered who was in Jeremy's room."

"Is something wrong?"

"Not really."

Next step. "I've got to do some research. Have we got all last week's newspapers, or did Dad put them out for the trash pickup?"

"I don't think he did," she answers. "They ought to be stacked up just inside the garage." I have my hand on the doorknob when she suddenly says, "And Del."

That stops me. "Del what?"

"You asked who was in the house. Del was when he came in for a drink of water."

"I know that, Mom. I meant anyone else."

She just shrugs, so I hurry out to the garage to get on with what needs to be done. I sit on the warm cement floor of the garage, the newspapers piled around me, and bless the small town reportage that covers every crime on the last page of the front section.

I read back through three days until I come to the story I think I'm looking for. The home of a Mr. and Mrs. Philip Dickery was burglarized on Wednesday. Among the items taken were a portable color television set, a small stereo radio, and some jewelry. The story gives the Dickery address, and I memorize it, feeling that's the safer way to do things. I check out the crime stories for the entire week, but can't find another "Phil"; so I put the stack of newspapers back the way they were.

Once more I check Jeremy's room for cufflinks, a ring, anything else that might be incriminating, but the only item that doesn't belong seems to be this watch. Philip Dickery's watch was put into Jeremy's desk drawer for a reason. Why? How does it tie in with what happened to Jeremy? For a few moments I press the palms of my hands against my forehead, trying to stop the ache of too many questions with no answers.

I'm sure of only one thing. If someone has a plan to hurt Jeremy even more, then I'm going to ruin his plan, because I'm going to return the watch.

Then I'll find out who did this.

The doorbell rings, and Mom's footsteps go trip-trapping across the entry hall. In a moment the door opens, and I hear her startled "The police? What is it you want?"

And there I stand, in the middle of Jeremy's room, with the watch in the pocket of my jeans!

CHAPTER EIGHT

The policeman says something to Mom. I can't hear him. But Mom shuts the door and her voice is so high and taut that it throbs. "Angie? Where are you?"

Slowly, I manage to walk into the entry hall and stand slightly behind Mom. Unless I turn around no one will notice the bulge in the back hip pocket of my jeans. And if I take long, deep breaths, maybe no one will hear my heart pounding.

The officer takes off his cap, leaving an angry-looking red band across his balding forehead, and rubs an arm across his face, blotting up beads of sweat. There are large, wet stains under the arms of his shirt. "Hot out there," he says.

"Oh." Mom reacts politely on cue. "Would you like to sit down? Would you like some iced tea?"

"Thanks, I sure would like some tea," he says. His glance skips around the entry hall and on into the living room. "I better not sit on y'all's good chairs. I've just got a few questions to ask."

"Angie," Mom says. "Will you bring the officer a glass of tea, please?"

They both look at me, and I take a couple of steps backward.

"Angie?" Mom says. "Some iced tea, please."

"Uh — sure," I stammer, taking another couple of steps. "Right away."

"Is there something wrong?" Mom asks.

Why couldn't she concentrate on the policeman? "No," I say. By this time I'm nearly at the entrance to the living room. In a couple of steps it will be safe to turn around.

Mom looks at me as though I'm creating problems, but the policeman concentrates on tugging a notebook from his shirt pocket. I make it out of the room. I shove the watch behind a stack of plates on the top kitchen shelf.

I bring back the iced tea, and the officer gulps it greedily, his head back, his cheeks puffing in and out with each swallow. Finally he gives a long sigh, hands the empty glass back to me, and turns to his notebook.

"Why do you need to know where Jeremy was going?" Mom asks.

"Just a matter for the record," he says. "It just helps us to fill out our information."

"I don't know what his plans were," Mom whispers, and she looks so lost that I hug her.

"Okay, then," he says. "Sorry to bother y'all." He stuffs his notebook into his shirt pocket and turns toward the door. "Thanks for the iced tea."

Mom closes the door and leans against it. "Angie, I can't believe that I didn't know where Jeremy would be that night."

"It's not your fault, Mom. I didn't know either."

She doesn't move. She doesn't answer. She looks so bewildered and vulnerable that I ache for her. So I add, "I'm finding out there's lots about Jeremy I didn't know, like his poetry."

Mom raises her head and looks at me blankly. "He reads poetry?"

"He *writes* poetry." I reach out a hand to her. "Come with me, Mom. I'll show you a book of Jeremy's poetry. It's pretty good."

I lead her into Jeremy's room. She sits on the edge

91

of his bed, gingerly, like a trespasser, and takes the notebook I hand her. She reads the first poem, then looks up at me, her eyes wide with wonder.

"I had no idea that Jeremy wrote poetry."

"Maybe we're intruding into his private life," I say, "but I don't think it's wrong. I think we should learn more about him."

She reads another poem. "His poetry is so sad," she says.

"I think he's writing about what he feels."

Her eyes were shimmery with tears. "He's lonely. I didn't know how lonely."

"Mom," I tell her. "Don't start tearing yourself apart over what Jeremy has written. Just read it and understand a little bit more about him."

The book lies open on her lap as she stares at me. "I don't know about either of my children. What about you, Angie? Do you write poetry too?"

"No, but I guess I feel somewhat the way Jeremy does."

She's still staring. "I don't know you. I don't know you or Jeremy."

I stoop down to hug her. "Hey, Mom. It's okay. I didn't mean to shake you up. I just thought you'd like to read this." I take the book from her and turn a few pages. "Here. Read this one. I think it's one of his best."

She obediently reads, and I say, "Mom, I'm going out for just a few minutes to run an errand. I'll be back soon." She just nods absentmindedly.

I'm going to take back the wristwatch.

Before I leave I fish out of my drawer some awful, huge sunglasses with mirror lenses that I wore the summer Meredith and I were sixteen and thought we were the greatest things to hit Malibu Beach since they invented movie stars. And I grab a faded scarf I should have thrown out a long time ago. The watch goes back into my hip pocket.

It's easy to find the right address. It's easy to find anything in Fairlie, because the town is so small. I have to smile as I think of the contrast with Los Angeles. Our car is the only one in sight, except for a couple of cars parked in driveways. I think of the L.A. freeways and the broad streets filled with traffic. A lot of people complain about all that traffic, but I wouldn't. You take the bad with the good, and the good is the city and all that it offers, all that it's going to offer to me next year when I'm at USC.

I pass the Dickery house. It's a fairly expensive, large, white-brick tract-type house with a neat little boxwood hedge outlining the front lawn. Good neighborhood. It's logical that Philip Dickery would own an expensive watch like the one in my pocket. I drive to the next street behind theirs. I can't just walk up and hand over their stolen watch. Would I ever have the police on my back if I pulled a trick like that! I can't put it in their mailbox or leave it on the doormat. I've got a plan in mind that I've got to make work.

I park the car, palm the watch, and put on the mirror glasses and scarf, tying it to cover my hair. I walk briskly around the corner and down the Dickerys' street, slowing as I near the house. I don't know who might be watching, so I've got to make this look good. I stop in front of the house and stare at a spot halfway up the walk, under their boxwood hedge. I like that hedge. It's going to come in handy.

After standing there for a moment I move a few steps up their walk. The front door opens. Great. I thought I'd have to do this alone, and now I think I'll have help. I glance up to see a little boy, about six years old or so.

"Hi," I say.

"Hi," he answers. "What do you want?"

"There's something shiny under your hedge," I tell him. "I noticed it glittering in the sunlight. At first I thought it was a garden sprinkler — something like that — but it's yellow, like gold. Do you see it?"

He looks at me suspiciously. "Where?"

"Right there. Look." I get to the spot at which I was staring before he can get down his porch steps. I kneel and reach in, under the hedge, coming up with the watch, which I dangle in front of him.

His eyes are wide. "That's my dad's watch!"

"It's a nice watch. He should have been more careful with it."

"Mom!" the boy yells. "C'mere quick!"

A woman who must go to the same hairdresser that my mother does comes through the open door and down the steps so fast that I scramble out of her way.

But she stops a few inches from me and glares at me as I stand up. "What's the matter? What's going on here, Jimmy?"

Jimmy hops up and down, narrowly missing my toes. "She found Dad's watch!"

The woman's eyes open wide as her frown seems to slide up her forehead and into her lacquered hair. I hand her the watch.

"It is!" she says. "It is the watch I gave Phil!"

Now she puckers into suspicion. It's like watching someone in a drama class trying to express a variety of emotions. "Where did you get this?" she asks me.

"Under the hedge!" Jimmy yells, before I can answer.

"Let her talk." The woman claps a hand on his shoulder, trying to hold him down.

"That's right," I tell her. "I was taking a walk, saw something shiny down there, and fished it out."

"I saw it too!" Jimmy shouts. "It was right down there! I saw it! I helped find it!"

Dear little Jimmy. He really did his good deed for the day. It might have been a lot tougher without him.

Now the woman is confused. "Oh," she says. She says it again.

That's enough conversation as far as I'm concerned. "I'm glad Jimmy found his father's watch," I say and turn to go.

But she takes a step next to me. "Please don't rush off," she says. "I suppose you're the one who really found it, and—"

"I helped! I found it too!" Jimmy interrupts. "I bet the burglars dropped it!"

Now I'm the one in acting class. I try to look amazed. "Burglars?"

"We were robbed Wednesday night," the woman says. "They took some jewelry — all sorts of things. And there is a reward for their return. I'm sure you must want whatever part of the reward my husband will give you for his watch."

"No," I say. "I just saw it, and Jimmy" — I beam at him — "Jimmy really found it. Didn't you, Jimmy?"

"That's what I keep telling you, Mom!" Jimmy yells. "But the reward—"

"I don't want the reward. Thanks, anyway."

I'm two houses away when she suddenly wakes up and shouts, "You didn't tell me your name!"

I just turn briefly, wave, and smile, and keep walking, pretending that I don't hear her. I keep up a brisk pace, and the minute I round the corner I pull off the glasses and scarf. I get into my car in a hurry and drive down to the main street. I pass a sterile, concrete shopping mall marooned in a nearly empty parking lot sea. It's an obviously new concession to the oil company employees and their families who have swollen this town, because on either side are the older stores, a few with the high wooden false fronts

I've seen in western movies.

Less than two minutes later a siren blasts behind me, and a cop car is close enough to hitch a ride on my rear bumper. I pull over to the curb, and the car parks behind mine. A policeman climbs out, so as fast as I can I shove the scarf under my right leg and tuck the glasses in my shirt pocket. They stick out of the top, but there's nothing else I can do with them. If that woman tells the police about a girl with mirrored sunglasses — if this policeman notices—

He turns around. I take a deep breath, which comes out in a shudder. "Is there a problem?" I ask.

"Let's see your driver's license," he answers.

I hand it to him and he copies some of the information from it onto his pad.

"Insurance identification?"

I give him the card. It's already in my hand. He takes it as though he's sorry I have it available. "Are you giving me a ticket?"

He doesn't answer, just keeps writing, so I say, "If I'm getting a ticket, I should know what for!"

"Sign here," he says, handing the pad to me, and in a monotone recites, "For one thing, your left taillight is out—"

"But it isn't!" I interrupt.

"If you don't believe me you can look for yourself."

I think about the scarf I'm sitting on. I can't get up, or he'll see it. "I'll take your word for it," I mumble.

But he stands back and waits. "Come on. I'll show you. You can tell your daddy to get it fixed."

"It's okay. Really. You said the left one. I'll tell him."

He pauses while I hold my breath. I can't let him see that scarf. Finally he turns back to his notebook. "And going forty-five in a thirty-five zone," he continues.

"I wasn't!"

"I clocked it, young lady."

"That's not true!" I guess I'm thinking slowly. I finally begin to get the message — back off, or there'll be more harassment.

"Sign," he says again.

I open my mouth to protest, but realize it won't do any good. So far he hasn't taken a good look at me. Maybe he's been too embarrassed to do so. My best bet is to sign that ticket and clear out as steadily as I can manage.

As soon as he's back in his car, I drive away carefully, thankful that it's over. My hands tremble on the steering wheel. This whole episode scared me more than I thought it would. As soon as I'm sure the policeman isn't following me I head down the nearest alley and stop long enough to stuff the glasses and scarf into someone's dumpster.

I told Mom I'd be back soon, but I've got such an urgent need to see Jeremy that I head for the hospital. Maybe Dad will still be there. I'm sure that Jeremy knows when one of us is with him. I hope he does, because I've got more to talk to him about.

I remember to look at the left taillight. The policeman wasn't kidding. It's not only broken. It looks as though it was smashed. There are a couple of small dents around the rim of the light. If I had backed into something I certainly would have known it. Maybe it was Mom. We both use this car. I'll ask her when I see her.

The hallways of the hospital rattle with dinner-tray carts, and a pungent, beefy odor from the tin-covered dishes overpowers even the pine-scented floors.

Dad is sitting in the chair by Jeremy's bed when I push open the door to Jeremy's room. A folder is open on his lap, and papers are strewn on the blanket. He takes off his reading glasses and stares at me for a moment before he recognizes me.

"Where are you?" I ask him. "Offshore Louisiana? Or ten thousand feet into Austin Chalk?" I pause. "Or here with Jeremy?"

"Angie," Dad says, "be flippant if you like, but I've got responsibilities. There's work to be done."

"No matter what happens." I finish the sentence for him.

He sighs as though he's trying to be patient. I guess he is. Gathering up his papers he manages to sneak a look at his watch. "It's about time to have some dinner, isn't it?"

"Why don't you and Mom go out?" I ask him. "I'd like to stay with Jeremy for a while. I can find something to eat when I get home."

"I guess we could do that." He looks relieved. "You're sure you wouldn't want to go with us?"

"You and Mom need some time together. And I'd like to be with Jeremy. Really. I would." I look at my brother, who still sleeps peacefully under that array of bandages and tubes. I think of the way his hand seemed to move in mine. "Does he respond at all when you talk to him, Dad?"

Dad looks startled. He stares at Jeremy, then back to me. "He's unconscious, Angie."

I'd like to talk to Dad about Jeremy, but I don't know how.

He stands, stuffing papers into the folder. "Mrs. Clark went out for dinner. She ought to be back in about half an hour."

"Who's Mrs. Clark?"

"The woman who is sitting with Jeremy today."

We stare at each other as though we're looking for loose pieces. "I'll stay with Jeremy until she gets back," I tell him. "Maybe longer. Don't worry about me. Okay?"

He plants a kiss in the direction of my forehead and

is gone. The rattling carts are muffled by the heavy door as it swings shut. I sit on padded plastic that is still warm and reach for Jeremy's hand. I wish I could talk to the woman in the newspaper story I saw, who read story books to her child when he was in a coma, and one day he woke up. Anything's possible. I've got to believe that.

"I went to the Andrews house," I tell Jeremy. "I think someone was there, but Del came too; and whoever was in the house left by the front door when we came in through the kitchen."

There's no response. I wait a few moments, then say, "Jeremy, is the Andrews house the one you wrote about? Is that where I'll find 'the ghosts of now'?"

Is it my imagination, or does he take a quick breath, out of time with his steady, rhythmic breathing?

"Jeremy, I am going to help you," I tell him. "I'm going to help you get well again, because I'm going to find out what happened to you and why. Do you hear me?"

Nothing.

My voice is low, almost a whisper, as I look at my brother, at his bruised face, the bandages immobilizing his body. "I love you, Jeremy." There are tears running down my face, warm salt trails sliding into the corners of my mouth. "Jeremy, I know I can get through to you! It's going to be all right! You've got to get better!"

I talk to him about discovering his poetry and how good it is. I go on about Mom unpacking his bird-house and how great it looks in the mulberry tree, and I tell him about Del.

Mrs. Clark stays away long enough to have a five-course meal and an after-dinner nap, but I don't mind. I'm happy being with Jeremy, and I'm happy because I was right. Some of what I'm saying is reaching him.

99

I feel it. And maybe some of what Jeremy wants me to know will reach me. So I don't just talk. I wait and listen and hold Jeremy's hand in mine.

But I don't pick up a message. Maybe I'm trying too hard. Every now and then the phrase "the ghosts of now" comes into my head, but at the moment it doesn't make any sense.

Mrs. Clark tiptoes into the room. It was good being with Jeremy, but I don't want to talk to her. I do a fast good-bye.

One thing about all that dust in the West Texas air: you choke on it, try to scrub it off, grit your teeth on it, and curse it, but it does make for spectacular sunsets. Gold and red have blasted the faded blue out of the western sky as I leave Jeremy in the placid care of Mrs. Clark. But by the time I get home the spectacular color has plopped out of sight and our unlit house is a solid blob in a darkening street.

I go through the back way, flipping on lights as though they're protection, uneasy at the silence in the house. Well, I told Dad to take Mom out to dinner, that I'd be okay. And I am. Nothing wrong. Is there?

For some crazy reason I check every room in the house as though I expect to find a burglar hiding in the closet. *Come on, Angie. Don't let this get to you.*

I wind up my tour in the kitchen. Wasn't there some pot roast left in a bowl in the refrigerator? If I slice it and some tomatoes and—

My head is in the refrigerator when the phone rings. It's like a shriek, and I jump. Maybe that's what's been wrong. Maybe I've been expecting this call. I close the refrigerator door and stare at the telephone on the kitchen wall while it rings again. *Answer it. Answer now. Get it over with.*

A third time the bell jars the silence. I find myself next to it, reaching for the receiver, holding it to my ear. "Hello?"

The whisper curls along my spine, sending out spasms of shivers. "Back off, Angie. You're only making trouble for your brother."

"Are you threatening him?"

"Be sensible, Angie. We have to protect ourselves."

"The watch?" I ask, and my laugh is as bitter as my hatred for this person on the phone. "If that's what you mean, forget it. The watch is no longer in Jeremy's desk."

But I'm talking to dead air. I'm not sure if the whisperer has even heard all that I said before he hung up.

I put the receiver down, trying hard to remember the voice. Was it a girl's voice? A boy's? Was there anything about it I could pinpoint?

No answer. No proof. Nothing. How can you tell who someone is when he whispers? But there was something a little different from the first time. A different voice? A different person? Maybe. The whisperer said "we." So now I know I'm dealing with more than one person. If I just knew who or why or what they were doing!

Someone knows. My hand is still on the phone, and Debbie's number is now in my memory, so I dial it. On the first ring Debbie answers.

"Was it you who just called me?" I ask her. "Are you the whisperer?"

"Don't do this to me!" she shouts.

"Threatening my brother isn't going to help you, Debbie."

"Leave me alone!" she screeches and slams down the phone.

It rings so quickly that I jump and pick up the receiver gingerly.

"Angie," Mom says. "I just wanted to check and

101

make sure that you're home and everything is all right."

"Sure, Mom." I hope she can't hear the wobble in my voice. "I was going to make a sandwich."

"Good," she says. The sigh of relief behind her word draws it out in a hiss. "Greg and I had dinner, and we're at the hospital now. We'll be here only a few minutes. I just wanted to see Jeremy again."

"Tell him you love him, Mom," I say. "Remember what I told you about how I think some of what we say reaches through. Tell him. It's important."

There's a pause. "I will," Mom says.

Suddenly I remember. "Oh, Mom, I almost forgot. Will you tell Dad that the left taillight is broken? I don't know how it happened. I didn't do it."

"Maybe a rock on the road. I broke a taillight like that once," she says. "I'll tell him."

"It looks like someone smashed it."

"Angie." Her tone is patient. "Who would do a thing like that?" I don't have an answer, so she adds, "Can we bring you anything?"

"No thanks. I'll find that leftover pot roast if I keep looking."

"It's in a bowl under the loaf of egg twist bread."

I make my sandwich, eat it, push back the empty plate, and fold my arms on the table, resting my fore-head against them. Because it dawns on me that the ghosts of now are not dead spirits — not yet. They are live, and they are more aware of me than I am of them. They have whispered their way into Jeremy's life and mine, and they're not through with us.

I won't give up until I find them.

CHAPTER NINE

Some of the kids I've met stop me in the hallway before classes and tell me they've read the newspaper story about Jeremy's accident, and they're sorry. It makes Monday a little easier to take. But Capped Teeth, whose name I've found is Candy and who seems to be Debbie Hughes's best friend, turns to glare at me when I slide into my desk before first-period class. Debbie's seat is empty.

With quick, pinprick glances she makes sure no one is aware of us and leans toward me. "You're stupid," she says in a low voice. "You don't know how stupid you are."

"Tell me why."

"I don't have to tell you anything."

"Except that I'm stupid? Where's your buddy?"

I nod toward Debbie's desk, and Candy knows who I mean.

She bares her teeth, her words a hiss. "Leave Debbie alone. You're making her sick. I mean like really sick."

"I want her to tell the truth."

Her laugh is more of a snarl. "No, you don't. You don't know what the truth really is."

"Then tell me."

But another bell rings, and stragglers swarm into the room. Del is among them, and he stops in the aisle between Candy and me, unwittingly ending our conversation. He leans down, resting both hands on my desk, his face close to mine. "How's Jeremy doing?"

"The same," I tell him. "Mom called the hospital early this morning, and they said there was no change. Mom's probably there right now."

He takes one of my hands and squeezes it, then swings into his desk, working to get his long legs tucked in out of the aisles.

Candy twists her head, flipping back her hair, and hands a thin, dark green notebook to Del. "Debbie asked me to give you this. She said you left it at her house last night."

Del doesn't reach for it. He just shakes his head. "It's not mine."

"Oh," Candy says. "She thought it was." She doesn't look at me, and I'm glad she doesn't, because I'm afraid my face must show what I'm feeling.

Our teacher sweeps into the room and raps on her desk with a broken ruler, and the class is under way. It's hard to concentrate. I keep reminding myself that Del can see anyone he likes. I have no claim on him. Just because he said— Never mind. Candy didn't answer my question. I'll ask her again after class.

But after class Del leans over my shoulder. "I can't read my own writing," he says. "Was that assignment on page 108 or 103?"

I straighten him out, and when I look up Candy has gone. I'll try to find her later. I don't understand what she said about my not really wanting to find out the truth.

I plod through the school day as best I can. It's hard to push my mind into chemistry symbols and French verb translations when it wants to be with Jeremy. At lunch time in the cafeteria one of the girls who had talked to me about sandstorms and living in West Texas waves a fork at me.

"Angie! C'mon over here and eat with us!" she says.

So I carry my tray to their table and climb onto the bench across from them.

"The yuck special again today," the other one says as she fishes into a bowl of macaroni and cheese.

I smile back. "Carol and Bobbie. Right?"

"You got it," Carol says. "It's always so awful having to remember so many new names when you change schools."

Bobbie pokes a straw into a bottle of orange drink. "It's gross for you having to be at school today. I know how I felt when my grandma was sick and in the hospital. I couldn't even think straight, because I was worrying about whether she'd die while I was in school, and—"

Carol jabs her in the ribs with an elbow. "Shut up, Bobbie. She doesn't want to hear about your grandma."

"I just want to tell Angie I know how she feels."

"But not like that." She quickly looks at me from the corners of her eyes. "I mean like somebody dying and all."

"But she didn't! At least not then she didn't."

"Bobbie!"

I lean across the table toward them. "Don't get unstrung. I understand what Bobbie's saying. And Jeremy isn't going to die. The doctor says his vital signs are good."

They both make enthusiastic noises and get back to their macaroni and cheese.

"Have you ever heard of ghosts in the Andrews house?" I ask them.

Bobbie drops her fork with a clatter on her tray. Her eyes are wide. "What's the Andrews house?"

Carol shakes her head and sighs. "Don't talk about ghosts to Bobbie today. She stayed up late to watch that awful movie on cable — that thing with the ghosts who turned doorknobs into faces and stuff."

"It was a good movie," Bobbie says. "I saw it three times the year it came out." She picks up her fork and licks off some gummy cheese strands. "So what's this about the Andrews place? Is that in Fairlie?"

"It's that old, run-down house at the end of Huckleberry Street. You know," Carol says.

"Oh, yeah," Bobbie says. "Some of the kids tried to do some witch stuff there last Halloween."

"But the neighbors called the police and they ran them off," Carol adds.

"I heard there were lights in the house, that people think there are ghosts there."

"Really?" Bobbie's eyes are as wide open as her mouth.

"Don't talk to her about ghosts!" Carol says. "She gets scared in the middle of the night, and then she calls me and wakes me up, and I can't stand it! There aren't any ghosts in the Andrews house, Bobbie! I mean it!"

"Sorry," I say. "I'll change the subject." I take a spoonful of yellow gelatin.

I guess I must have made a face, because Carol says, "It doesn't matter what color it is. All of it tastes the same. If you don't want it, I'll eat it."

But I'm hungry, and I eat everything as fast as I can. It goes down better that way. Finally I swing my legs over the bench and pick up my tray. "I have to go to my locker and get my books for this afternoon," I tell them. "Thanks for asking me to eat with you."

"Any time," Carol says.

"Yeah," Bobbie says. "Like tomorrow. We mean it."

Carol tears an end off a piece of paper in her notebook, scribbles something on it, and holds it out to me. "Here's our addresses and phone numbers. Mine's at the top. Why don't you come by after school today?"

"I better go to the hospital after school," I tell them. "But thanks a lot. That really helps. I'd love to come some other day. Okay?"

"Sure," Carol says.

"And if you find out any more about ghosts—" Bobbie begins, but Carol slaps a hand over her friend's mouth.

I'm still smiling as I shove my tray of dirty dishes through the collection window, but someone pushes a little too close, a body tight against my side. I try to move away, but a voice in my ear says, "I have to talk to you."

I whirl to look directly into Boyd Thacker's eyes.

He says again, "I have to talk to you. C'mon outside on the front steps."

"Why not?" I follow him out of the cafeteria almost eagerly, as my excitement grows. I'm going to get some of the information I want. I know it!

He doesn't say a word as we thread through some clusters of people in the hallway. He flings one of the front doors wide and goes through. I manage to catch the door before it slams in my face, and push through to join him.

Boyd stands at the side of the steps, next to a chipped pillar, and leans against it. He doesn't look at me until I say, "Well? What's on your mind?"

"It's hard to talk about," Boyd says. His eyes are on the houses across the street as though they're the most fascinating things in his life. "It's terrible to tell a girl something about her brother that she really wouldn't want to know."

"Boyd!" I move a little closer, grab his shoulder, and shake it. "Look at me when you're talking to me!"

He turns, but his eyes are so dark I can't attempt to read what's behind them. "I didn't want to tell you

107

what happened to Jeremy Friday night, but — well, some of us think you ought to know, so you'll leave Debbie alone. You've got her so upset she's sick in bed."

"Now, wait a minute! It's not my fault if Debbie's sick!"

He leans closer. "Do you want to hear what I've got to tell you or not?"

It's hard to stay calm. "Yes."

"Okay. Then listen. We had a party."

"Where?"

"Just listen to me. I'll tell you what I can."

"Okay. Go on."

"Some of us got together for a party, and don't ask me who was there, because I won't tell you. And don't ask where it was, because I won't tell that either."

I clamp my teeth together to keep from saying a word.

"Anyhow, it was at this girl's house, because her parents were out of town, and a lot of us had too much to drink, and somebody took Debbie's car."

I can't help it. "Who?"

"We don't know. There were some kids from another town at the party — word got around — and we think it was one of them."

"Jeremy was at the party too?"

"Yes. Only he got real moody. He had some stuff to drink, and maybe he couldn't handle it. In any case he's not much fun at a party, or maybe you know that. He started talking about how life didn't mean much to him, how it would be a lot easier if he were dead."

"No!"

"I told you that you wouldn't like the truth. Now you've got to hear it. Anyhow, Jeremy ran out of the door and down Avenue G toward Huckleberry, and I didn't—"

"Which direction on G?" He looks blank for a second, so I say, "South or north?"

"What difference does that make?"

"I need to know."

He frowns. "Okay. He was running toward the north, I suppose. Anyhow, if you're through interrupting, I'll tell you that I didn't want to go after him, but I felt responsible, because I brought him to the party, so I did. He acted like he didn't know what he was doing. And he ran right into the street. Didn't even look. This car was coming fast down Huckleberry, toward Avenue G."

I interrupt. "From the dead end block of Huckleberry?"

He scowls at me. "No. Of course not. The other direction. I guess the driver didn't see him in time, because the car didn't stop."

"Debbie's car?"

"No. I don't know whose car it was. I heard that the guy who took Debbie's car cracked it up against a tree. This was someone else, and I was so busy trying to find out if Jeremy was killed or not I didn't pay attention to the driver or the license plate or anything."

"Are you the one who phoned me?"

He shakes his head sorrowfully. "No. I just ran back to the house and called an ambulance."

"You should have stayed with him."

"I came back to check on him again. He was breathing all right. Look, some of those kids were pretty drunk. Some of them were stoned. We couldn't take any extra chances. We turned out the lights and waited for the ambulance to show up. We knew they'd do anything for Jeremy that could be done."

"You were home when I called you."

"That's right. Most of us got home as fast as we could manage."

"And you lied to me. You said you didn't know where Jeremy was."

"I wasn't thinking. I was scared. I didn't know what else to do at the time."

"But you're telling me this now."

"Because you're pushing. A lot of kids could get hurt if you keep this up, Angie. Some of them might lose scholarships, or get kicked off the team."

"You think I believe that you care so much about them?" I glare at him with pure hatred.

"We stick together," he says. "We've known each other all our lives."

A bell over the front entrance clangs jarringly. Boyd shifts his weight to the balls of his feet as though he's ready to leave, but I block his way. "One more question. What do you know about a watch?"

His eyelids give the faintest flicker, but his gaze is steady. "I don't know anything about a watch. Did Jeremy lose his watch? Is that what you mean?"

When I don't answer he puts a hand on my shoulder. "Angie, I don't think you understand what I've been trying to tell you. It's pretty obvious to me that Jeremy wanted to commit suicide."

CHAPTER TEN

"I don't believe you!" But some of the lines of Jeremy's lonely, desperate poetry bounce off the walls of my mind and send shudders down my backbone.

I push them away and take a step closer to Boyd, my face almost against his, but he doesn't flinch. "There's something else you're not telling me. I think you put a man's wristwatch in Jeremy's desk. It was stolen in a robbery, and you have to be the one who put it there. I don't know why you did that. So tell me!"

"Where is the watch?"

"Back where it belongs."

"What are we talking about then? A watch that doesn't exist?"

"I found it in Jeremy's desk drawer."

He smiles. "But now you can't prove there was a watch, can you?"

"I — I guess not."

He sidles away from the pillar, moving back. "I told you what you wanted to know. What's the matter with you, Angie? Why dream up a lot of other junk?"

Suddenly he looks upward, to someone beyond me, and a strange look flickers across his face so rapidly that I can't read it.

A voice interrupts my thoughts. "Angie," Del says. "I saw you out here." He puts an arm across my shoulders. "How you doin', Boyd?" he asks.

Boyd says something, which is drowned out by the clanging of the bell, and hurries back into the building.

The hot breezes swirl little eddies of dust across the steps and against my legs. I rub my arms, feeling the sun and the grit on my skin. But I'm cold, and I shiver.

"Angie?" Del asks. "Are you okay?"

I can't answer, and he turns me so that I'm facing him. "Did Boyd say something that got you upset?"

"I don't want to talk about it now."

"Sure," he says. "But you've got to go to class. I'll walk you there."

He propels me inside the door, and somehow I get through the rest of the afternoon. As I leave my last class I find Del standing in the hallway outside the door, waiting for me.

"I'll give you a ride home," he says, taking my arm.

"Thanks, but I can walk." I try to pull away, but he holds fast.

"Nope. Something's bothering you, and I'd like to know what."

"It's my problem, not yours." He waits, and I add, "I mean you know the way I feel about Debbie, and if you're dating her—"

"Oh," he says. "What Candy said about last night."

A couple of people, hurrying in the opposite direction, elbow against me, pushing me into Del. I stumble, but Del steadies me. With an arm around my shoulders he moves me through the hall, down the steps, and out to his pickup truck in the school parking lot.

He leans down, and his face is very close to mine. "I've known Debbie since we were in kindergarten," he says. "And we dated for a while. It didn't work out, but in a way we're still friends."

"It's none of my business," I stammer.

"Yes it is. It's because of you that last night she

112

called and asked me to come over. She wanted me to tell you to leave her alone. I said I already had. I told her you were kinda stubborn."

His slow smile gets to me. Without any pretense I say, "When I heard that you were at Debbie's last night I was jealous."

Del doesn't answer. He just takes my shoulders, pulls me toward him, and kisses me. It's a light kiss, a quick kiss, one that kids moving their nearby cars out of the lot wouldn't even notice. But it shakes me.

"Now," Del says, "I'll take you home."

Something has been growing in my mind like a little fungus in one of those time-lapse films they show in science classes, and as I climb into the car I say, "Del, could you take me to the place where — you know — Huckleberry Street and Avenue G?"

Without asking any questions he simply says, "Let's go."

On the way to our destination I fill him in on what Boyd told me about the party.

"I can't believe what he said about Jeremy deliberately running out in front of a car," I tell him.

"Could be Jeremy didn't know what he was doing if he had too much to drink," Del says. "He's under age. It may have been the first time he had any hard liquor. It could have hit him pretty hard."

"But there's something that's bothering me."

"What?"

"I'm not sure yet."

Del eases his pickup over to the curb on Avenue G, and I just sit there, staring at the intersection. According to what Boyd told me, Jeremy ran into the street at Avenue G, going north; and the car was coming down Huckleberry from the west.

It's like the answer to an impossible question on a pop quiz suddenly coming into your head, or a puzzle

113

with the pieces showing up in the right place. I open the door on my side of the truck and jump out, running to the spot. I hear Del following me.

"Angie? What are you doing?"

Now I'm sure. "Boyd was lying to me. If the accident had happened the way he said it did, Jeremy would have run across the street here and have been hit by the car from this side. Wouldn't he?"

"I guess."

"Then his injuries would have been on his left side. But it was his *right* side that was hurt so badly."

Del frowns as he thinks. Finally he says, "Maybe. But what if Jeremy suddenly saw the car coming and turned around? Lots of things could have happened."

"That's not the way Boyd told the story."

"He probably wasn't too sure what he was doing either. Look, these parties happen, Angie. Jeremy shouldn't have been there, but that's after the fact now. Why don't we go to the hospital and see how he's coming along? That makes more sense to me than standin' here tryin' to play detective with all the odds against you."

"My brother didn't want to kill himself."

Del is talking to me, but I tune him out, because my mind is being tugged in another direction. I raise my head and stare down Huckleberry to the end of the street. There's just a glimpse of yellow brick set back from the street behind the ragged curtain of overgrown, untended shrubbery, only a portion of the house that is overshadowed by its nearer, more tidy neighbors. The Andrews place.

In my mind I am walking up the front steps toward the draped windows that are like hooded eyes. But the eyes are opening, and there are mouths with lips moving, stretching, twitching, contorting! Screams no one wants to hear! The ghosts of now!

Del grips my shoulders. "Angie? What's the matter?"

Like an echo I hear the whimpering sounds that have been coming from my mouth.

I lean against Del, shaking, shivering, trying to steady myself. "I'm sorry. Something frightened me."

He pats my back clumsily. I can hear his heart thumping, and I put one hand against his chest, as though I can soothe the heart back into its normal rhythm. "It's that Andrews place," I mumble. "The ghosts—"

I can't finish the sentence, but it doesn't matter, because Del twists to look in that direction and says, "You can hardly see the old house from here. You just let your imagination go crazy."

"I'm sorry, Del. I didn't mean to scare you." I back off and take a couple of deep breaths to steady myself.

"You didn't scare me. I just didn't know what was happening to you."

"Could you drop me off at the hospital? I want to see Jeremy."

"I'll come in with you."

"No. Not yet. I'd rather be alone with Jeremy until I get things sorted out."

"How will you get home later?"

"Mom might be there at the hospital, or I can call Dad for a ride on his way home from the office."

He tilts his head, shoving back his hat, and studies me. "You're sure you're all right now, Angie?"

I try to smile. "I'm sure."

"Okay," he says, takes my hand, and leads me back to his truck.

Del doesn't ask any more questions, and I'm glad, because I don't want to tell him the rest — the part about the watch. Maybe because it's too much of a

115

puzzle, and I can't figure it out.

The door to Jeremy's room is closed, and I open it slowly, quietly, disappointed when I poke my head inside and find that Mom isn't there.

The gray-haired woman in the chair by the bed smiles at me without missing a stitch, her knitting needles tickety-tacking at a great rate.

"How are you, Mrs. Clark?" I ask automatically.

"I'm Mrs. Burrows," she answers. "Mrs. Clark's not on duty tonight."

Someone has taken the second chair away, and Mrs. Burrows is as settled on hers as a fat little robin on her nest. So I put my books on the little table by the wall and stand at the foot of Jeremy's bed.

"If you want to leave for a while, I'll stay with him," I tell Mrs. Burrows.

"That's sweet of you, dear, but I'd better stay on duty."

"I can take care of Jeremy."

"But it's my job." She smiles. "There's really nowhere I'd want to go. I'm settled in and comfortable, thank you all the same."

I can either leave or try to pretend Mrs. Burrows isn't there. I choose the latter. It's important to talk to Jeremy.

"Hi, Jeremy," I say. "It's me — Angie."

Mrs. Burrows's smile twists into a grimace of sympathy. "Dear, he can't hear you."

"He can hear me."

"But he's unconscious. It's as though he's sleeping. Sleeping people can't hear what's said to them."

"Sometimes they can. There's such a thing as sleep learning. People play tapes to listen to while they're asleep."

116

The needles never stop. "I hadn't heard of that, dear."

"Jeremy," I say, ignoring her, "I love you."

Mrs. Burrows sighs. "You're such a nice little family. It's obvious that you and your brother are very close to each other."

I squeeze my eyelids tightly shut, trying to blot out the burning tears that push against them. A few escape down my cheeks, and I angrily rub them away with the back of one hand.

The door opens and a voice behind me says, "May I come in?"

I turn to see a man with thin white hair, his shoulders rounded. His hand that curls around the door is gnarled with large, blue veins.

"My name is Gerald Clary," he says. "I don't want to bother you. I just came by to see how the boy is doing."

His sudden presence has wiped out my tears. I sniffle away the last of them and nod. "Please come in. I'm Angie Dupree, and this is my brother, Jeremy."

He nods and bobs, even at Mrs. Burrows, whose name I've forgotten. "You're Mrs. Dupree?" he says.

"No," she says. "Doris Burrows," and she gives him her broad smile.

"I've called the hospital a number of times, but they don't want to tell anybody anything; so I thought I'd come by."

"That's very nice of you," I say.

He ducks his chin to peer over the bottom part of his bifocals, examining Jeremy. "That was terrible," he murmurs. "Just terrible. Is he sedated?"

"I don't think so," I answer, as Mrs. Burrows — authority in her voice now — says, "No. He's still unconscious, but his vital signs are good."

What does that mean? I want to shout. But I quietly

wait until Mr. Clary asks, "Is the doctor hopeful about the boy?"

"Yes," I answer. "We just have to wait."

"My wife stayed with him until the ambulance got there," he says. Then he adds, "We didn't know who he was, who else to get in touch with. The ambulance driver said he didn't have any identification, and he was all alone."

I turn to stare at him. "You mean you were there when the car hit Jeremy?"

"Not exactly," he says. "I guess I didn't explain. My wife and I heard a squeal of brakes. We were still watching TV, and I ran outside, and there he was" — he waves a hand toward Jeremy — "lying there in the street. The car that hit him was nearly a block away, and I couldn't give the police any information about it at all."

His face is puckered, and the little grooves around the corners of his mouth turn down in concern. "My wife ran out and put a blanket on the boy," he says. "And I'm the one who called the ambulance."

"So you were there just a few minutes after the accident happened."

Mr. Clary nods. "More like a few seconds. I can still move pretty fast."

"Was there anyone else on the street?"

"No one," he says. "What with the street lights and a good-sized moon, I would have seen anyone who was on the block. The only one there besides my wife and me was whoever was driving that car."

118

CHAPTER ELEVEN

I thank Mr. Clary for his kindness to Jeremy. My mind is working on two levels at once. I know I'm saying all the right things in response to what Mr. Clary is telling me, but at the same time I'm picking my way through jagged edges of lies that snag my thoughts, holding me back from finding the truth.

Finally he leaves, and I hurry to the man at the admittance desk.

"Could I ask you a question?"

He looks up and smiles. "Hey, sis, I remember you. How's everything going with your brother?"

"He seems to be the same. Please. I need to find out something."

"Sure, sis," he says. "What's on your mind?"

"Someone called an ambulance for my brother. Would you have a record of that?"

"Not us. The police."

"Thanks." I go back to Jeremy's room and use his phone. Mrs Burrows watches me closely, but I try to forget she's there. It doesn't matter.

It takes a few minutes to find the right person to speak to when I call the police. The operator who finally talks to me has more questions than I have.

"Yes, we do keep a record of who calls," she says. "But that's not exactly public information — unless there's a good reason. Why do you want to know?"

"I — uh — want to thank whoever called," I say.

Mrs. Burrows looks up quickly. I turn my back on her, so I can't see her.

"Oh," the police operator says. "Well, that's nice, I guess. Just a minute."

She comes back with the name of Gerald Clary. Even his phone number.

"Was he the only one?"

"That's the only name we've got."

"If someone else called, too, would you have that name?"

"Sure."

"I mean, if Mr. Clary had already called, would you just tell the other person 'never mind' or something like that and not take his name?"

"We record every call that comes in. It's on tape as well as written down." She sounds a little antagonistic.

Something else occurs to me. "What if the call was anonymous?"

"It would still be recorded. I thought you said you wanted to thank the person who called in. Just what are you getting at?"

"Nothing," I say quickly. "I just wanted to know who called. Thanks a lot for your help."

I press down the button on the phone, hold it just a second, then lift it to get a dial tone. I dial the operator and ask for Dr. Crane's office.

Someone is in the middle of telling me that Dr. Crane is not in and she'll take a message when the doctor himself walks into Jeremy's room.

I simply hang up the phone and turn toward the doctor. "I'm so glad to see you," I say. "I have an important question to ask you."

He takes off his glasses and squints at me as though I were a bug. Then he says, "I'll take a look at my patient first, if you don't mind."

Dr. Crane checks Jeremy's chart, then takes his

pulse. He lifts Jeremy's eyelids and bends nearly into his face as he stares into his eyes with a little light. He keeps doing all the things I guess doctors must do. Finally, he nods to himself, makes a notation on Jeremy's chart, straightens, and looks at me.

"How is Jeremy?" I ask.

"You're his sister?"

"Yes. How is he?"

"No changes, to speak of."

"When will he wake up?"

"That we can't say."

He twiddles with the stethoscope that hangs over his dull brown business suit and moves toward the door.

"Wait, Dr. Crane. I need to ask you something important."

He stops, takes off his glasses, rubs his nose, and puts them on again. "I thought I had answered your question."

"No. Not this one. I need to know if — well, if Jeremy had been drinking before he was brought to the hospital."

He frowns. "You think he had been drinking? Your brother is pretty young to be drinking, isn't he?"

"Jeremy's friend, Boyd, told me he had been at a party, that he'd been drinking. I don't think he — that he was right, and I need to be sure. Would you have by any chance checked to see if there was alcohol in his blood?"

"We would have checked, and not just by any chance, young lady. We're very thorough here, just as we would be if we were in a big city."

I suppose I can't blame him for being irritated about Dad bringing in a specialist. Maybe I'd feel the same way if someone thought my work wasn't good enough. But he shouldn't take out his grumpiness on me.

"Was there any trace of alcohol?"

121

"No," he says. "No trace of alcohol at all."

"Thank you."

I'm speaking to his back as he goes through the door. Okay. I've found out what I needed to know. Boyd's story was nothing but lies, and I don't know why. And I don't know where to look for the truth. If only Jeremy could tell me.

Mrs. Burrows gives a little sniff. "It's none of my business, of course," she says, "but it looks as though you're deliberately trying to get a very nice boy into trouble."

"What?"

I blink at her, watching her lips press together and open again before she adds, "It doesn't really matter who said what or why, does it?"

"I don't understand this conversation."

"Probably not." Her knitting never stops. "But when you say 'Boyd,' everyone in town knows you mean the Thacker boy, and what's the point of suggesting that he tells falsehoods?" Without a pause she says, "He mows my lawn in the summer, y'know. Lovely boy."

"I'm not trying to get anyone in trouble," I tell her. "I'm just trying to find out what happened to my brother."

She doesn't answer. I turn and gaze down at Jeremy with the same strong feeling that there are answers I need to find in order to pull him back. And I can't talk to him. Not with Mrs. Burrows here.

It's not quite time for Dad to leave his office, but I call him anyway.

Mrs. Burrows makes a little humming noise in her nose and says quietly, as though she's talking to herself, "They charge fifty cents for each phone call."

Dad answers, and I tell him where I am and ask if I can get a ride home.

"I'll come over right away," he says. "We're at a standstill here, and I'd like to see Jeremy." There's a pause. "I suppose his condition hasn't changed?"

"No."

His voice sounds tired as he says, "I'll be there in a few minutes, Angie."

He *is* there in just a few minutes, but he doesn't want to stay. He sort of pats in the direction of Jeremy's toes, makes some small talk with Mrs. Burrows, and leads me out of the room.

Dad's got something on his mind, and I'd feel like an intruder to break in, so for a while we don't talk. Finally he says, "Angie, there's something strange going on. Maybe you can tell me why."

I turn to look at him, and he adds, "This afternoon our land department got word from the bank that they won't cooperate on some right-of-way leases that up until today looked as though they'd go through with no problems."

"I don't know anything about right-of-way leases."

"No, but you do know that Grandy Hughes is president of the bank."

"I don't understand."

He sighs. "Never mind, Angie. I shouldn't have brought it up. It couldn't have anything to do with —"

His voice trails off, and he's back into his thoughts again. I hate this town. I can't wait until next year, when I'm back in California.

As we come in through the kitchen we hear voices in the direction of the living room. Someone is babbling on, with a chorus of giggles in the background.

Dad and I look at each other.

"I guess Mom's got company," I say.

"That's good," he answers, his words rising as though they're on a musical scale. "I'm glad that she's got someone with her."

123

I follow him into the living room. Mom is there, leaning back against the deep cushions of the sofa. She has kicked her shoes off, and she waves a glass in our direction. "There's Greg!" she says to the two women with her. "You know Greg." She giggles. "And my daughter, Angie, whom youm don't know."

They all think that's terribly funny, and I can see that anything anyone said would be terribly funny. There's an empty Scotch bottle on the coffee table, along with an almost full one and a shiny aluminium ice bucket that's sweating and dripping all over the table.

Mom sits up straight after a couple of tries. "Mrs. Dunlap and Mrs. Grein — my daughter Angie."

"Hi," I say.

Mrs. Dunlap squints through a film of cigarette smoke that's the same gray-brown as her hair. She takes her cigarette from her mouth, smiles, and murmurs something, but Mrs. Grein bats her fake eyelashes at Dad and says, "My goodness, Greg, if you're home from work already, then I'd better get home and make dinner for Jake!"

"It's a little early," he says. "I stopped by the hospital to pick up Angie and see Jeremy."

Immediately both women's faces twist into serious expressions. "We came by to try to cheer up Barbara. That was a terrible thing. Simply terrible," Mrs. Grein says.

"We'd better go," Mrs. Dunlap says. She stubs out the pink-smeared butt of her cigarette into an already filled ashtray and heaves herself out of her chair and onto her feet.

Mrs. Grein fumbles inside her handbag for her car keys, dropping them a couple of times as she digs down for a glasses case. Finally she tucks her sunglasses on her nose and her handbag strap over her shoulder. She gets to her feet and holds out a hand to Mom.

It's anyone's guess which one of them needs steadying the most. They sort of hold each other up, reminding me of a rag doll dance some kids did in a talent show when I was in seventh grade.

"Maybe I'd better drive you home," Dad says, and Mrs. Grein gets coy again.

"Now, Greg, don't look so serious. We just had a couple of little drinkie-poos." I'm about to gag when she adds, "Nothing that would interfere with my driving. Evelyn isn't worried about my driving, are you, Evelyn?"

"Not any more than usual," Evelyn says, and the three women laugh hysterically.

By this time we've all reached the front door. "Thanks again for coming," Mom tells them. They hug her again as they leave.

"That's not going to help," Dad says. He frowns down at Mom, who curls her lip in a little pout.

"Don't be so stuffy, Greg," she says. "I had to be so-sociable." She has trouble getting the last word out, so she frowns, too, and adds, "Besides, it *does* help."

"You're drinking too much lately," he says.

Mom stands up so stiffly that she loses her balance and puts out a hand to steady herself against the wall. "Oh? You mean you've been counting? Hmmm?"

Dad doesn't answer. He just turns and walks out to the kitchen.

"I better make dinner," I tell her. My voice comes out as cold as Dad's had been, and Mom blinks at me. I didn't mean to sound that way, but I can't help it. For a few moments I wish I hadn't come home at all.

"Angie," Mom says, and she clutches my shoulders, looking into my eyes. "You and Greg — you just don't understand."

I don't know how to answer her. Maybe I don't understand. Maybe I don't want to. But I think about Jeremy. I don't know any more about Mom than I do about him. "I thought you'd be at the hospital with Jeremy," I blurt out. "You weren't with him when I got there after school."

Mom's shoulders sag, and her voice is high, like a little girl's. "I sat with Jeremy most of the morning, and he slept. He just slept, Angie."

Her fingers tighten on my arms, and the pressure hurts. Instinctively I step backward, pulling away. "I'd better do something about dinner, Mom."

"Angie, I did what you said. I told him that I love him."

I'm still walking backward. "That's good, Mom." Her face is crumpling, and she starts to cry.

"He didn't move. He didn't answer me. I don't think he heard me at all."

"Oh, Mom! Don't do that, Mom!"

"Angie!" Dad calls. "Where the hell is the bread knife?"

I turn and run toward the kitchen.

Dad is standing in the center of the kitchen, his hands at his sides, looking as uncomfortable as a pedestrian caught by a light change in the middle of rush hour traffic on Wilshire Boulevard. If I ever get married, my husband is going to have to know how to cook.

"We could have sandwiches, I suppose," Dad says. "Do you know what we've got on hand for sandwiches?"

"I'll fix something," I tell him. I put a hand on his arm. "Why don't you talk to Mom? I'll call you when dinner's ready."

"Not now," he says, and he drags a chair from the table, screeking it across the floor.

"She was crying."

His mouth tightens, and he leans against the table, his hands against his chin in that gesture I know so well. "Leave it alone, Angie."

I pull out the rest of the leftover pot roast, slice it, and put it in a pan with some bottled barbecue sauce to simmer. I open a can of string beans and chop some lettuce, tomatoes, and green pepper in a bowl for salad. All this time Dad doesn't say a word. He sits at the table, staring at nothing. I wonder if he's thinking about Mom or Jeremy. I know he doesn't want to talk, but I need to. And this seems like the right time, so I sit across the table from him, where he has to look at me.

He still doesn't say anything, so I blurt out, "Dad, I don't think you've noticed that Mom's awfully lonely."

He blinks a couple of times, staring at me. "I'm sorry, Angie. I'm trying to work out a problem. I didn't hear what you said."

"A problem about Mom?"

Again he looks at me as though he's on a different plane entirely. Then he shakes his head. "This is a personnel problem, something at the office I've got to handle before tomorrow."

"Dad, I was trying to tell you about Mom. She's lonely."

"Lonely? I don't think you know what you're talking about. She has you children. She has me."

I think of how I felt when I had to say good-bye to Meredith. Was it like that for Mom each time she moved away from friends? "Maybe that's not enough for Mom," I say, and I know it's the wrong thing when the lines under Dad's eyes sag and he looks as though I've struck him. "That's not what I meant," I tell him. "I was thinking about friends, and —"

But Dad shoves back his chair and stands. "You

127

don't know what you're talking about," he repeats.

I watch him stride from the room, his back as stiff as a toy soldier's, and I smell the sticky-sour sauce that is scorching into bitter blackness on the bottom of the pan.

I turn off the stove and stir dressing into the salad. "Dad," I yell. "Dinner's ready."

No one answers, so I walk back through the house. There's a murmur of voices coming from the open doorway to their bedroom. Mom blows her nose, and her voice is heavy with drips and hiccups.

"Dinner's ready," I repeat.

"We heard you, Angie. Thank you," Dad says.

I don't want this, and I don't want dinner. I get my handbag, fishing out the car keys, and head for the door. There is something else I've got to do. Once in a political science class our teacher said, "In an argument look for the weakest link. That's where you'll be able to break through."

In this situation I know where the weakest link is. Debbie. It's time to talk to her, face to face.

But Debbie's face is not what I get.

I hear heavy footsteps coming to her front door, thudding across the polished wooden floor in the entry hall. The door swings open, and I look eye-to-eye at a short, slightly pudgy, balding man who has eyes like smooth, round stones. If this is Debbie's father, she's lucky she looks like her mother.

"Mr. Hughes?"

"Yes." There's no uplift of question in his voice, as though he doesn't care who I am.

"May I please speak to Debbie?"

"Debbie's not here."

"When will she be back?"

"Not for a week or so. She went to visit her aunt in Lubbock."

Over his shoulder I see Mrs. Hughes, craning her neck as she tries to peer out the door. I hear a muffled "Oh!" when she recognizes me.

"I'm Angie Dupree," I tell him. "May I please come in? I had wanted to talk to Debbie, but maybe it would help if I talk to you and Mrs. Hughes."

His eyebrows move together like two caterpillars in collision. Mrs. Hughes squeezes close behind him, whispering in his left ear. Only one word comes through, and that is "no."

"You're trying to cause a lot of trouble, young lady," he says. "Do you realize how much damage you've done?"

"I don't want to cause any damage," I tell him. "But I must find out what happened to my brother." The door is moving toward its frame, an inch at a time; so I quickly add, "Maybe everything will work out if I can just get the answers I need. I've found out some things that probably involve Debbie, but if you won't talk to me, I'll go back to the police."

"Hold on a minute," he says. The door swings almost closed, and I hear vague mumbles and mutters behind it as Mr. and Mrs. Hughes discuss what I've said.

It slowly opens wide, and the two of them stand there, glaring at me. "Come on in," Mr. Hughes says.

If it weren't for Jeremy I'd run, but I've got to find out.

I step inside and follow them across the entry hall, past the wide staircase, and into a paneled den complete with built-in gun rack and a coffee table with an orderly row of *House Beautiful* and *Ladies' Home Journal*.

I follow the direction of the hand Mr. Hughes has flung out and sink into one end of a love seat. They perch opposite me on a matching love seat.

"Well?" Mr. Hughes asks, so I try to tell them what happened, including most of what Boyd told me.

"That's all it was!" Mrs. Hughes squeals like the tires on an old car coming to a fast halt. "It was a party! Just a harmless little party!"

Her fingers fumble with the neckline of her dress, and she calms down a bit, adding, "Oh, we know the kids are too young to drink, but after all, everyone does it, and all the kids in Baby's — Debbie's — crowd are good kids."

"That wasn't a harmless party. My brother was hit by a car."

"It wasn't Debbie's car, if that's what you're getting at," Mr. Hughes says.

I shrug. "You had Debbie's car fixed in a big hurry. Then you sent the mechanic out of town on a vacation."

Their eyes meet as though little magnets pulled them together. He quickly looks back at me. "Where did you get that information?"

"It doesn't matter. It's true, isn't it?"

He gives a long sigh. "Listen to me, Angie. That night some of Debbie's friends dropped her off at home. She woke us up and told us about the party. She said it had got out of hand, and there were a few kids who drank too much."

"Not Baby, though," Mrs. Hughes interrupts.

"And she told us there had been some party crashers, and one of them stole her car."

"She was terribly upset. What her father isn't saying is that she was really ill from crying and carrying on. Our Debbie isn't the kind of girl who could tolerate a party like that."

Mr. Hughes puts a hand on his wife's knee, and she clutches it with both hands. "I called the police and reported the car stolen. Y'all talked to the police, so you know that."

And apparently they reported my visit to him. "What time did you call? Before or after the accident?"

"Does it matter?"

"Only that it could have been Debbie driving the car, and the story about its having been stolen might not be true."

Mrs. Hughes's nostrils quiver and her lower lip juts out. "Are you trying to make us believe that Debbie didn't tell us the truth?"

"I'm trying to find out the truth."

Mr. Hughes leans toward me, his hands clenched, his elbows resting on his knees. "Debbie's always been a good girl," he says. "She's pretty and popular and has lots of friends."

I have to ask. "What does she think about? What does she talk about? What is Debbie really like?"

"What a silly question," Mrs. Hughes says.

Mr. Hughes frowns again. "She's like all young girls her age," he says.

It's just what I thought. They don't really know their daughter. She's living in the same house with them, and they talk to her every day, and her mother calls her "Baby," and they just don't know. Not any more than in my family.

But now it's my turn, and I try to get a bead on Mr. Hughes's stone eyes. "If you were really sure that Debbie was telling you the truth, you wouldn't have been so quick to take care of her car."

"I don't like your suspicions, young lady," he says. "And I don't like what you're doing — trying to hurt some fine kids who've grown up together in Fairlie, who'll come back here to live and raise their children and help Fairlie continue to prosper."

Mrs. Hughes quivers as she interrupts part of his leftover Chamber of Commerce speech. "You outsiders — y'all have no right to come in here and disrupt

131

our lives! And you particularly — you have no right to upset Debbie the way you've been doing!"

We're at a stand-off. And the only thing I've learned is that Debbie has lied to her parents. Because I'm beginning to believe that on that horrible Friday night there was no party.

CHAPTER TWELVE

Dad and Mom are sitting at the kitchen table drinking coffee. I feel like a fool for tiptoeing through the back way so quietly.

"I know," I say. "I should have left a note. But you were talking, and I was upset, and—" I shrug. "Okay. I should have left a note to tell you where I'd be."

"You can't just walk out of the house like that," Mom says. "Especially when it's dark."

"We were worried," Dad says.

But they're still cradling their coffee cups, and their voices are smooth with exhaustion, the aftermath of an argument that's been settled. I'm glad they worked things out. I wonder if Dad tried to find out what Mom is feeling.

"Where were you?" Dad asks.

I sit down with them at the table, and brush away the cup Mom moves toward me. "I've been talking with Debbie's parents."

They wait for what I'll say next, so I tell them about what Debbie told her parents and what Boyd told me.

When I finish, Dad just sits there, staring like some kind of zombie. Mom rests her forehead against her hands. "Dear God!" she whispers.

"And it's all a bunch of lies," I say.

She lifts her head and looks at me. "I read Jeremy's poetry too. There is a lot of despair in it."

"I don't believe that Jeremy wanted to kill himself. And he hadn't been drinking. I asked the doctor, and they didn't find alcohol in his blood."

"But Boyd said—"

"Mom, there are some kids who have worked out a lie for their parents, and their parents are busy kicking sand over that lie to cover it up so they won't have to see it's really a lie."

"Why?" Mom looks so confused I put my hand over one of hers the way I would with a small child.

"Now, Angie, we don't know there's been a cover-up," Dad says. "You don't have facts. You're just guessing. Adults have to deal with facts. It sounds as though you've been watching too many detective shows on television."

"I'm not guessing. I'm trying to get the facts."

"I still don't understand," Mom says. "Why would Boyd tell you that Jeremy had been drinking, and the doctor tell you they found no alcohol in Jeremy's blood? Is there something else involved?"

I don't want to tell them yet about the stolen watch. I don't know why. It's just a feeling I have, so I keep quiet.

Dad puts down his cup and gets to his feet, walking to the sink and back a couple of times before he says, "Angie, we don't belong in Fairlie. We'll move on from here, just as we've always moved ahead in the company. In a way I agree with Debbie's father. Why should we stir up problems for the people who have made their lives in this town? All we should be concerned about is helping Jeremy to get well."

"That's why," I say, and he stops to study me.

"I'm trying to reach Jeremy," I tell them. "I have a strong feeling that if I know what happened, I can talk to him about it. I'm not sure of the reason, but I suspect he isn't trying hard enough on his own, and maybe if he knows that we understand and things will be made right, it will help bring him back."

Mom's fingers tighten around mine. "I've tried talking to Jeremy, honey," she says, "but he doesn't hear us. He's unconscious. You have to realize that."

So I tell them what I told Mrs. Burrows about sleep learning and about the newspaper story I read last year of the child in a coma whose mother kept talking to him.

Dad shakes his head. "That's pretty far-fetched, Angie."

But Mom says, "Honey, if you think it will help, then do talk to Jeremy."

Dad turns to Mom. "Dr. Branning will be back on Wednesday. They may make some tests."

He and Mom begin to talk about tests and hospitals and doctors in Houston, but I tune them out. I think of my brother, and I know I'm going to summon every ounce of strength I've got to try to reach inside that dreamworld into which Jeremy is locked and bring him back. I can't give up without trying.

But will I be able to do it?

The question haunts me all evening, and when I lie in bed ready for sleep it hangs over my head. I'm at that point where thoughts become fuzzy and unreal, making a slide into sleep, when it happens.

The wall behind the headboard of my bed thuds as though a giant fist has hit it. I scream and leap out of bed as the blow slams again.

Mom and Dad scramble down the hall and into my room.

"What is it?" Mom screeches.

But Dad throws open a window. "Hey, you!" he yells. As I rush to the window with Mom I see some shadows scrambling over the back fence.

Dad's voice is tight and deep. "I'll see what damage

135

they did," he says. "They must have been throwing something at the house."

He strides from the room. Mom and I sit on the bed, just looking at each other. Finally I say, "Whoever it was must have known which was my bedroom. They were trying to scare me." I add, "And they sure did!"

Mom pats my hand. "What makes you think they're after you?"

But Dad is back. He holds out his right hand. His fingers are stained a dark red.

Mom gasps, and I shout "Dad!"

"Tomatoes," he says. "They threw tomatoes against the wall."

"Tomatoes? But they made so much noise!" I giggle with relief that it wasn't blood.

"Should we call the police?" Mom asks.

But I shake my head. "They won't do anything."

Dad adds, "There's nothing they can do. Whoever was in our yard has gone and we couldn't identify them."

"Why did they do it?" Mom asks.

They look at me, but I only shrug. Maybe they've figured out, too, that whoever did it knew which room was mine, that this was aimed at me. But I guess it's easier not to say what we've been thinking.

Finally Dad says, "Let's get to bed. I doubt if they'll come back."

I lie in bed staring at the darkness, listening for sounds I hope will never come. I'm sure I won't be able to sleep again, so I'm surprised when my alarm clock wakes me.

Carol and Bobbie are waiting for me in the hall at my locker when I get to school. I stuff in some books, the backs of my fingers rubbing against the grit of fine sand that has sifted through the cracks around the metal door.

Automatically I rub my hand down the side of my jeans, and Bobbie nods. "Wait till the wind really starts to blow, and everything you eat feels gritty. Yech!"

"How's your brother?" Carol asks.

"The same," I answer. I wish I could tell them what I'm trying to do with Jeremy, but they might think it's dumb, just as Dad did. I don't know them well enough to want to find out.

The bell blasts from over our heads. Bobbie claps her hands over her ears. "We'll go with you to visit him, if you'd like," Carol adds.

We begin to walk down the hall, dodging our way through the people who all seem to be hurrying toward us. "I'd like that. When he's a little better, maybe." I'm shouting at Carol, who's now a couple of feet behind me. Bobbie's pushing along behind her.

Some big oaf, who's probably fullback on the first string, shoves between us, nearly flattening me against the wall. Carol waves and calls, "See you at lunch!" and she and Bobbie are swept down the hall.

The door to my first-period class is a few steps away. It's a safe spot for now, a place away from hurrying, shoving bodies. A place where I'll see Del.

In a way I'm surprised at the warmth that spreads across my shoulders like an extra sweater when I look across the room and catch Del's smile. He's been talking to Candy, but he quickly moves away from her and toward me, and I know he's been watching for me to come through the door.

"How are you?" he asks, his voice so quiet that only I can hear him. I know he's asking if I've come to terms with the status quo, if I've ended the fight.

"I think I'm a little closer to the answers now," I tell him. For a moment I think I see a sadness in his eyes, and I don't understand it. "Del, will you help me?"

"You know I will," he says. When he smiles I

137

realize I must have only imagined the sadness. Del puts an arm around my shoulders and we walk to our desks. My eyes meet Candy's for just an instant, and this time the anger in her glance is not there, just a curious, speculative look. There's something going on that I don't understand. It's a disturbing feeling that clings through the rest of the day.

At lunch time Bobbie slaps her tray on the cafeteria table and swings her legs over the bench. "My mother sent off a check for my housing next year!"

"Where?" I ask.

"A and M," she says. "It's a terrific university." She scoops up a large bite from a baked potato.

"Where are you going to college?" Carol asks me.

"University of Southern California," I answer. Just hearing the words aloud brings such a rush of excitement that I shiver.

Bobbie says, "You ought to go to A and M with us. You'd love it, and you'd still be in Texas."

"I'd rather be in California." I forget about the stuff on my lunch tray as I tell them about Meredith and what we have planned.

"It sounds terrific," Carol says.

"Awesome," Bobbie says around a mouthful of food.

"Most of the kids go to A and M or Texas, and some go to SMU, and there's always Tech up at Lubbock and the out-of-state universities," Carol says.

"Everybody goes away," Bobbie adds.

"What about the junior colleges around West Texas?" I ask.

"Sure," Carol says. "A lot of people go to them for their first two years. The ones who can't go away to school."

I had driven past one of the junior colleges — fairly new modern buildings on a campus near the edge of town, where students can glance out windows and see the flat desert, covered with scrub to the horizon, all of it dusted gray with a shifting, sifting layer of dry earth.

"They've got some good teachers," Carol says.

"But it's lots nicer to go away to school," Bobbie adds.

For some reason this conversation disturbs me too. Maybe it's just the day. I don't seem to be with it. Everything is crowding in — too many thoughts, too many problems to handle. I'm relieved when the last bell rings.

I begin the short walk home. By the end of the first block the people going to their cars have dropped off, and only one or two wander on in my direction, but today I'm aware of footsteps behind me. I've got the scary feeling that something is wrong; so I whirl around. Close to me are five kids. Four of them I've seen but don't know. The other is Candy. I've stopped, and they stop too.

"What do you want?" I wish I could sound calm. They must know they've frightened me.

"We just want to talk," Candy says slowly. A couple of the kids shift position. A guy moves to my left. A girl moves close to the right, jostling my books out of my arms.

I try to gulp down my fear. "You want to talk about what happened to my brother? Is that it?"

"Let's talk about your not being so nosy," Candy says. "You say too much to too many people, and it gets back to us." She steps forward and kicks at my books, sending my English book skittering across the dusty sidewalk.

"Cut it out!" I have to step backward as they move in on me.

"You don't belong here," one of the guys says.

139

I try to brace myself. I don't know what's going to happen next, but I'm not going to take it without a fight.

I'm suddenly aware that a blue pickup is coming down the street fast. It screeches to the curb, and Del jumps out.

He walks steadily toward the nearest guy. "Something I can do for y'all?" His words are a drawl, but the tone is hard and strong.

"Forget it," the guy mumbles. He turns around, and the others follow.

"Don't try this again," Del says. They don't answer as they walk back toward the school.

He picks up my books, then turns to me. "Taxi service to the hospital, ma'am." He makes a bow and points toward his pickup, parked at the curb.

"I'm so glad you're here!"

He smiles, but his eyes are serious. "I'll stick around a little closer from now on."

"You don't have to."

"Of course I don't. I want to."

He opens the door, and I climb up and in, leaning back against the seat, wishing I could close my eyes and sleep.

Del is beside me, watching me, one hand on the ignition without turning the key. "You look kind of pale," he says. "My aunt Bessie would say, 'downright peak-ed'."

"What's 'peak-ed'?"

"The way you look now."

Del starts the truck, pulls away from the curb, and doesn't speak until we're a couple of blocks from the school. "Did you have to read *Don Quixote* in the school you were in last year?"

"Tenth grade."

"Okay. So you know how he kept fighting wind-

140

mills — trying to set things right when there was no way he could win."

"You think that's what I'm doing?"

"I *know* that's what you're doing. Angie, give it up. Let things be. We're talking about a bunch of kids at a party that got out of hand."

"But you helped me, at first. You even found out about Debbie's car."

"I figured if you got some answers to all those questions it would satisfy you. How would I know you didn't understand what to expect in a place like Fairlie?"

The sun glares against the windshield. I close my eyes, because they hurt. "We're talking about hit and run," I say. "That's a crime. And I think the crime was committed with Debbie's car."

"There's no way you can prove that."

I lean back, away from Del. My words come out sharper than I mean them to. "You can tell Debbie you tried hard, but I wouldn't buy it."

"I don't have to tell Debbie anything. Remember, I told you the way it was in small towns before Debbie ever asked for my help. I'd like you to drop this thing that's got you so unhappy, so we can relax with each other." He attempts a smile. "Remember, I promised to teach you country-western dancing."

"I'm sorry, Del, but I've got to find some answers. I keep thinking about that old house and 'the ghosts of now,' which I haven't found yet, and I feel somehow they're tied in to the rest of it."

Del drives into the parking lot of the hospital, turns off the ignition of the pickup, and turns, with his back to the door, to look at me. "What are 'the ghosts of now'?"

I start at the beginning. I tell him about Jeremy's poem, and I tell him about the web of lies spun by

141

Debbie and Boyd, with the stolen watch caught in the middle like a fat, gleaming spider.

When I've finished, Del says, "But now you can't prove there was a watch."

His words are too much like Boyd's. I sit upright, one hand on the door lock, wishing Del had said anything else. "I've got to see Jeremy."

"Think about what I've said," Del tells me, and he bends over and lightly kisses my lips. His skin has the warm, sour-spicy fragrance of sunbaked grass, and for a few moments I don't think. I forget. Closing my eyes I eagerly return his kiss.

A nearby giggle from someone passing by trickles through the open windows, breaking the spell. I've got to get away from Del. My feelings about him are so strong, so muddled that I just want to be alone.

"Remember what I said, Angie," he calls, as I jump from the pickup and shut the door.

I don't want to remember. I run, my shoes kicking up a shiver of dust as I hurry into the hospital building.

CHAPTER THIRTEEN

Mom is seated by Jeremy's bed. A gray exhaustion seeps through her immaculate makeup, and in spite of her smile the outer corners of her eyelids droop. I kiss her cheek and nod to the placid guardian who is plumped into the chair on the other side of the bed. "Hello, Mrs. Burrows."

"Mrs. Clark, dear." She waves a waggling knitting needle at me. "Mrs. Burrows was on duty yesterday."

"How was school?" Mom asks.

"Okay," I answer. "Had a quiz in French. I think I did all right."

I'm sure she doesn't hear the answer. She might not even know what she asked. I think that particular question is programmed into Mom's brain and pops out each afternoon whenever she sees Jeremy or me.

We chat for a few moments, the three of us, saying nothing, talking trivia, until I can't stand it any longer. "Why don't you both go down to the cafeteria and get some coffee?" I ask them. "I can stay with Jeremy."

"Well," Mrs. Clark says, wrapping her knitting around the needles and tucking them into a large bag next to her chair, "I suppose I *would* like to stretch my legs."

Mom looks into my eyes, and I realize she's more aware than I thought she was. She knows I want to talk to Jeremy. "Good idea," she says, and she straightens up from her chair, stretching and rubbing the back of her neck.

They leave, and the room is quiet. Down the hall people are chattering, and every now and then a buzzer sounds at the nurses' station. But our white-walled cocoon is set apart, and here I can try to reach Jeremy.

For a few minutes I just study him. He looks a little thinner, but his legs stretch to the end of the narrow bed, and I realize how tall he has grown. The bruises that show are yellowing, and I know that means he's healing. I take his left hand and hold it carefully.

"Jeremy, I found a gold wristwatch in your desk drawer. Maybe Boyd put it there. I don't know. And I don't know why he did. But I took it back to the people who own it before there could be any trouble about it."

Maybe it's the way I'm lightly touching his fingers. Maybe it's just my wishful thinking. But I feel a current running through our hands, an electricity joining us together. "Jeremy, everything is going to be all right. I wish you could tell me what happened Friday night, but since you can't I'm going to find out anyway."

I think of what Boyd said about Jeremy's depression. I don't believe Boyd, but what Jeremy had written told of his loneliness. So I talk about that.

"You're not the only one who's lonely," I tell him. "We've all been lonely. It's awfully hard to leave friends. It's hurt Mom too. And maybe even Dad. He's probably been too busy to notice, but someday it might catch up with him. But we're a family, Jeremy. We have each other. And I'll be here with you. I'll be a real sister to you, for a change."

I wait, and his hand now rests heavily in mine. "The doctor said you have to fight to get better, Jeremy, so

144

you've got to try. I'll help you. Please try."

I will Jeremy to respond. I lean toward him, and with all the intensity in my mind and body will him to come back.

But the door flies open, and Mrs. Clark says, "That little snack did me a world of good, dear."

Mom is behind her, and she says, "I went grocery shopping this morning, and got a package of chicken breasts for dinner. Angie, if you wouldn't mind making dinner, you could take my car — it's in the third lane in the parking lot — and Greg can come by this evening and pick me up."

"Aren't you tired, Mom? I could stay while you go home for a rest."

"Neither of you has to stay," Mrs. Clark says. "That's why I'm here, and Jeremy's coming along nicely."

"The doctor did another brain scan this morning," Mom says. "Everything looks good." She gazes down at Jeremy and adds, "But he won't wake up."

"Sometimes it takes time," Mrs. Clark says. "And medical science never knows how and why. I sat with a patient one time who was unconscious for nearly a year."

"Really," Mom says, and I can tell that her mind has mercifully tuned out Mrs. Clark.

I give Mom my chair, say good-bye to Jeremy, and head for home.

As I walk in the door I shiver. The air conditioner has made the house a little too chilly, and the quiet in each room is just as cold. I make a clatter, on purpose I guess, dropping my books on the kitchen table, scuffling my feet, moving noisily inside the swirling dust specks that glitter in the afternoon sunlight to turn the controls down a little.

Maybe I sense it. Maybe I've been expecting it.

When the telephone rings I know who it is. The whisperer.

There's a strange sound to the call. I can't put my finger on what it means. But I'm sure this voice is the same as the first voice I heard. And the voice is shaking, crying, as it says, "You must stop. Now! Or you're going to be sorry."

"Why?" I demand, more angry now than frightened.

"Listen to me! I don't want anybody else to be hurt!"

"Then tell me! What really happened to my brother?"

But the whisperer begins to sob and breaks our connection.

I stand there with my hand on the phone. This call, with its strange, hollow quality, was more a warning than a threat. And why —?

With a rush of remembrance I realize what that sound was — the almost-echo that sometimes comes with long distance calls. So someone not in town has called me. Debbie, who's in Lubbock, staying with her aunt? That was more than just a ghostly voice. It must have been Debbie.

"The ghosts of now" flood into my mind, and I'm positive that I must make one more trip to the Andrews place. When Del and I searched it we didn't look in the upstairs rooms. I don't remember why we didn't. Was it Del or I who decided to leave? But what if one of those rooms holds the answer I need?

Automatically I begin to dial Del's phone number, but something stops me. I don't understand what I'm feeling. I detest the idea of going to that Andrews house alone, but at the same time something is telling me not to ask Del to go with me.

I don't have time to figure this out. I check my watch. It's too early to start dinner now. If I hurry I'll get back in time. It's easy to get into that house through

146

the back door, and on this trip I'll know the way.

I stuff my driver's license into a back pocket of my jeans, and scoop up the car keys with trembling fingers. I've got to follow my plan before fear can gobble up my determination.

I drive to the alley in back of the house and park there. I don't want anyone to see my car on the street. But I've checked Huckleberry as I passed at the corner, and there are no other cars in sight. I pick my way through the weeds, over the dried, cracked, uneven ground, and carefully climb up the cement steps, past the broken screen door, across the cracked linoleum on the porch, to the back door.

Gingerly I clamp my sweating fingers around the door knob and turn it. It moves easily, and the door swings open. I step inside the old, shadowy kitchen and close the door silently behind me. I am terrified of this house, but at the same time I don't have the creepy sensation I had the first time I was here, that someone or something was watching me. The ghosts who live in this place are not here now. The old house and I are alone.

I move through the rooms as quietly as an intruder can, my legs wobbly, my hands shaking as I grasp the banister. Up the stairs I climb, slowly, feeling the old wood bend, hearing it groan under my feet, snapping into place behind me with the sound of ghostly footsteps.

At the top of the stairs I pause. The doors are open at either side, and I catch glimpses of yellowed, tattered wallpaper, flowered patterns that withered years ago. I go down the hall to my right, peering into bedrooms with dusty, sheet-draped furniture, bathrooms with brown-stained fixtures. And I find nothing.

So I try the left side of the hallway. It's shorter, and it ends in a much larger room than the other bedrooms. Its windows, with torn, yellowed shades, open from the back of the house onto that untended garden. It's an L-shaped room, apparently planned as bedroom and sitting room. I lean against the door frame and gasp as I see a radio, a couple of cameras, and other odds and ends piled on the torn and faded green satin chaise, and the mounded shapes of two portable television sets on the floor beside it. And they're not old and dusty. They were put here recently.

There it is, laid out for me. The answer. Or part of the answer, at least. Stolen property.

Wispy wraiths that float through haunted houses do not steal television sets. The ghosts of this house have bodies with hands to snatch and legs to run and minds to know what they're doing. Who are they? Debbie? Boyd?

Jeremy?

"No! Not Jeremy!"

The spoken words shatter the silence, frightening me so much I cry out and make a rush for the stairs. I tear out of the house in a panic, flinging myself through the door and down the steps and across the yard, gasping for breath with a pain so intense I have to rest my head on the steering wheel of the car and make myself relax before I can drive home.

I'm glad the police aren't following me now. I don't mean to, but I drive through two boulevard stops and nearly hit a car parked near the corner of our house. I pull into the driveway, remembering as I throw open the car door to put on the parking brake, and stumble into the kitchen where I flop into a chair, hanging onto the table until the shaking stops.

Finally I'm able to pull the pieces of my mind together; and while I try to think I cook, browning the chicken breasts in some melted butter, adding a little celery salt and onion salt and lemon juice, covering the pan and putting it on simmer. I start the brown rice, which must cook for forty-five minutes, and wonder if we should have a vegetable. Who cares about vegetables? All I can see are those things piled on the chaise and on the floor next to it.

And where does Jeremy fit in?

The idea doesn't come in a rush. It's been there in little pieces like those in a jigsaw set, fitting together in bits and chunks until it begins to form a whole. I had wondered about the watch. If someone had planted it in Jeremy's desk, then there should have been a follow-up, some kind of threat. And no one has seemed afraid of what Jeremy might say or do when he regains consciousness. Scratching at the back of my mind has been this terrible feeling that Jeremy himself put the watch there. I have to admit to myself that when I first opened his desk it would have been easy for me to miss it. Now I let the thought come through, examining it, flinching at the pain. Jeremy is the one who stole that watch.

I'll go back to that house, and I'll wait for someone to come, even if I have to wait every night for a week. I think the person I'll wait for will be Boyd, and I'll demand to know what really happened. I'll demand that he tell me how Jeremy is involved. And I won't accept any more lies.

The phone rings, scaring me so much I shriek. Not the whisperer. Not now. I couldn't take it. I'm tempted not to answer the phone, but it might be Mom or Dad. So on the fifth ring I pick up the receiver, clear my throat, and manage to say hello.

"Angie," Del says. "I was fixing to hang up. I thought you might still be at the hospital."

My relief comes out in a long sigh.

"You okay?" Del asks.

"Sure," I say. "I'm okay. I was just starting dinner."

"Are you a good cook?" There's a teasing in his voice.

I try to match it, but my voice is coated in lead, and it won't float. "Sometime I'll show you."

"What are you cooking? I might angle for an invite."

Why not? There's plenty of chicken. I'm about to invite him to dinner when he adds, "I didn't call to get asked to supper. I thought I'd take you to the Andrews place tonight."

It's like getting socked in the windpipe. I have a hard time gathering words together. Finally I'm able to blurt out "Why?"

"You said you wanted to go."

"I did?"

"Sure," he says. "In the car. Don't you remember?"

But I don't remember. I'm sure I hadn't thought of the plan until later.

Suddenly I'm afraid of Del. I've trusted him to help me, but phrases come back, dangling strings of words that keep telling me to forget, to back off, to leave it all alone. What has he really been saying? *Now you know this much it ought to satisfy you. Stop pushing for answers, because you can't win.*

Has that been Del's unique way of warning me?

Who are the people who have haunted the Andrews house? Is Del one of them? And why does he want me in that house tonight? I don't know who to trust. I'm scared!

"Hey, Angie, are you there?"

I gulp and say, "I don't want to go there tonight, Del. Some other time. Maybe tomorrow. I've — uh — got to study for a test tonight."

"Okay," he says, and his voice is so easy and sure of itself that I'm more frightened than ever.

"I-I've got to go," I stammer. "The chicken is burning."

150

"A real good cook, aren't you?" Del chuckles, and I hang up, blotting out the sound.

I lift the lid of the pan, poking at the chicken pieces with a long-handled fork, trying to convince myself the chicken really was sticking and I wasn't lying to Del. Maybe I'm becoming paranoid, not trusting anyone. Had I said something to Del about the Andrews house, about wanting to go there? I don't remember everything I say. I must have.

I'm telling myself to be rational, but at the same time a trickle of hysteria shivers through my mind.

Slapping the lid on the pan I pick up the telephone. I'll end the problem here and now by calling the police.

The receiver is at my ear, the dial tone humming monotonously, when I realize that it won't help at all. Look what happened when Jeremy was hit. No one did anything. So what if they find all that stolen stuff in the Andrews house? What will they do? If the police have been protecting the old families here in Fairlie, where will that leave Jeremy? And the answers to my questions?

No. I've got to find those answers myself.

It's hard to eat dinner and talk to Mom and Dad and go through all the motions of being a normal person, when I'm not. At one point during dinner Mom asks if I'm feeling all right, and I tell her I've just got a lot of stuff on my mind. Well, it's true.

It's not quite dark when I come in with my set of car keys and a notebook and tell them I'm going to the library.

"When will you be back?" Dad asks.

"I'm not sure," I tell him. "I have to look up some things for history."

So the squared, one-floor library with the small windows and the narrow aisles between the stacks is my first stop. There are other kids I recognize using

151

the same reference books I'm after.

Forget it. I'm not going to wait. It's time now to do the rest of my errand.

I drive to Huckleberry Street just as it's turning dark, and the visible sky is only a narrow slash of red on the west horizon. I park near the corner, hoping anyone who sees the car will think it belongs to the nearest house. I pull a large, shiny flashlight out from under the car seat.

No one is on the street as I walk quickly toward the Andrews house, cut down the drive behind it — stumbling a little in the dark — and go inside.

I listen, but there are no other sounds in the house besides those I have made and the creaking of the old lumber. Cautiously, I turn on the flashlight, keeping the beam down and low as I climb the stairs, trying to ignore the wavering shadows that seem to clutch at me. My heart is thudding as I enter the room at the left end of the hall.

Someone has been here. Most of the things that were piled on the chaise are gone. One small television set remains on the floor, a camera strap draped over it, a cassette player next to it. Obviously, someone has been taking the stolen things away. And he'll return for the rest.

There's a small spindly-backed chair against the wall, almost behind the door. I can sit here and get a good view of the door. I can see anyone who enters before that person sees me.

So I turn off the flashlight, shaking until my eyes become accustomed to the darkness, and wait.

CHAPTER FOURTEEN

Shapes begin to form: the ragged splotches of sky around the torn window shades — sky just a shade lighter than the thick darkness in this room — the mound of the huge, old bed, the stretched-out lump of the chaise. But there are lights and shadows I can't identify.

"Angie."

The whisper slithers through the room, coming from a form that slowly raises itself from behind the chaise. I'm out of my chair, on my feet, before the hiss slips away. My flashlight is shaking — or is it me? — but I'm finally able to turn it on and throw the beam toward the chaise and whatever is behind it.

Boyd is standing there, squinting against the light. He throws up a hand to shield his eyes, and I lower the beam. "You're hard to scare. I thought you'd tear out of here," he says.

I'm glad he doesn't know how frightened I am. I try to keep my voice from wobbling. "The things that were in this room" — I hold out my left hand toward the television set — "they're stolen, aren't they?"

He ignores the question and says, "I told them you'd be back. I was right."

Now that I know I'm dealing with Boyd and not a nameless fear, my heart has stopped banging against my ribs and is settling into its own rhythm. "Where are you taking these?"

He smiles. "To a playground. We're stacking them all under the swings, where someone will find them." He pauses. "With fingerprints wiped off, of course."

"Why?"

"Why not?"

"Can't you take them back to their owners?"

"Open and honest, like you were when you took back the watch that Jeremy stole?"

I just shrug.

"We wouldn't have to do this at all if it weren't for you sticking your nose in."

"Why did you steal these things?"

"We were bored."

"And you got Jeremy involved."

He moves to the chaise and flops astraddle. "It wasn't hard to get him into it. But he's a creep."

I take a long look at him. "You're telling me that once he got in he didn't want to stay in. Right?"

"A creep," he says again. "He has no sense of adventure."

"It wasn't a party he was running from. It wasn't hard to figure that out. He was running from this house. Now tell me why."

"It would have been a good joke," he says. "But your brother wouldn't go along with it. The rest of us have done it, but he wouldn't. Robbing his own house, that is."

"What did you do with the things you took? Sell them?"

"Nope. Kept them. We never took much. It was the game that was exciting." He leans toward me, his black eyes glittering. "The fear of being caught, the tension, wondering if the people who lived in the houses would suddenly return home, the safe get-away. That was the great part."

He swings his left leg over the seat of the chaise,

so that he's facing me. "And you ruined it for us, Angie."

"It's a dumb game," I tell him. "It's not a game at all. What you've done has hurt people."

He slowly gets to his feet.

"And Jeremy," I add. "You went after him when he ran from here, didn't you? You panicked, because you thought he'd go to the police."

I think for just a moment. Maybe it's the closed-over look in his eyes that tells me the real story. "*You* were driving Debbie's car, not Debbie."

"It was an accident," he says. "Jeremy suddenly turned and ran into the street."

"Why didn't you stay with him? Why didn't you help him?"

"Debbie was coming apart. I had to get her away from there." Boyd pulls a lighter from his pocket and fiddles with it. "She's still a basket case. Scared to death of what you're going to do."

"I know. Debbie is the one who called me after Jeremy was hit." I think about the last call. "She phoned me again — today — to warn me."

"Besides being a basket case she's an air head."

"You tried to warn me too. Weren't you the other whisperer?"

His mouth twists into what looks like a smile. "You're awfully stubborn."

I'm so intent on our conversation that it takes me a moment to react when Boyd suddenly stares at the open doorway.

I whirl to see Del, and an ache rushes into my throat. "Not you, Del," I murmur.

"You told me you didn't want to come here." He sounds puzzled.

I just shake my head. I can't answer him. Tears will spill out instead of words.

"You know that if you say anything about this, Jeremy will be liable too," Boyd says to me.

"You're all cowards — all of you who are in on this." I can't look at Del. I don't want to look at him ever again.

"There's just a few of us," Boyd says. "But enough, and we know what we're doing. It really wouldn't matter what you'd say, because it would be your word against ours. And not a scrap of proof. And just to make sure you don't tell some wild story about this house —"

His arm sweeps wide, the flame from his lighter a red flash. I lunge toward him without thinking, screaming "No!" and we fall across the chaise, banging against the floor, Boyd under me.

But I'm too late. The flame swoops up the nearby brittle window shade, splashing itself across the wall, exploding in loud crackles and choking, acrid fumes.

Hands are tugging at my shoulders, strong hands that jerk me to my feet. "Get out of here!" Del shouts.

But Boyd doesn't move.

"You knocked him out," Del yells at me, and he stoops to grab Boyd under his arms, shoving the smoldering chaise out of the way, dragging Boyd across the floor.

"Take his legs!"

I do, and we stagger through the hallway and down the stairs, coughing and choking, racing the smoke and flames.

The front door stands open, and we stumble through. My foot catches on the lower step, throwing me forward, off balance, and I drag Del down with me, landing in a heap on top of Boyd.

Boyd groans, coughs, and stares up at us, shouting "Get the hell away from me!"

A burning shingle bounces near us, and we scramble.

Del hangs onto my arm as we dash into the street. Boyd runs a few steps from us and turns. "And you, you stupid kicker!" he shouts at Del. "Don't you try to do anything either!"

He's down the street and in his car before what he has said sinks in. I'm struggling through guilt and relief, but Del's strong hand is here, and I hang on.

People are rushing out of their houses, and we can hear the whine of the fire sirens coming closer.

Del just grabs my elbow and steers me through and around the people who are gathering. No one pays attention to us. They're intent on the burning house.

I don't look back. I keep walking until we're standing beside my car.

"You shouldn't have come here by yourself." It's the first time I've seen Del angry.

"Why did you come?"

"Because you sounded strange on the phone. And I know how you feel about this house. When I called back, and you weren't there, I was pretty sure where I'd find you."

"Oh, Del!" I wrap my arms around his neck, wondering how my crazy mind could have mixed him up with all of this. My tears are wet between our cheeks. He tilts my chin upward, then holds me tightly. His kiss is long and warm and firm against my lips. For a while I forget about everything except Del.

When we move apart his voice is a little deeper, not as strong and steady as it usually is. But he's as responsible as ever. "You drive home," he says. "I'll be right behind you. When I see that you're safe inside, I'll go on."

I don't want to let go of his hand. "Del, come in with me."

"No," he answers. "I think you've got things to tell your parents about Jeremy that need family privacy."

He opens the car door for me. For a moment I think he's going to kiss me again, but he takes a step back and smiles. "Hey, Angie, we'll get together again — soon."

I smile back. "Very soon."

It's difficult to do, but I start my story at the beginning. I sit across from Mom and Dad in the living room. When I've finished I wait for them to say something. Anything.

Finally I break the awful silence. "We'll have to tell the police."

Mom's voice is so soft I can hardly make out the words. "That might mean Jeremy will be arrested."

"Maybe, but I don't think so," I tell her. "They can't arrest Jeremy and no one else."

"But —"

"They won't arrest Debbie and Boyd and the other kids who were involved in that so-called game. They won't dig for proof. Not if it's going to upset those fine old Fairlie families."

"Honey, you sound so bitter."

"Maybe I am, Mom. I guess I've found out that life isn't always fair."

Mom looks to Dad for help. "Greg, what should we do?"

Before he has a chance to answer I say, "I think we should also let Debbie's parents and Boyd's parents know what's going on."

Dad shakes his head. "Do you think they'd listen to you? Did Debbie's parents believe you when you talked to them before? They'd rather not know the truth."

"But they're going to hear it — from us and from the police. Then it's going to be their problem, not ours."

"Our problem is that Jeremy was involved. We

have to accept that." Dad stares at the floor. Is he talking to us or to himself?

"Maybe—" Mom clears her throat and tries again. She's been hanging onto Dad's hand until her knuckles are white. "Maybe — after Jeremy's better — he could — uh — get some help."

"Help?" Dad turns to her. "I'm not sure what you mean."

"Counseling? Uh — maybe a psychiatrist?"

"Forget that," Dad says. "We can take care of Jeremy's problems ourselves. Only the physical problem is serious. He just got in with a bad bunch of kids. If — when he's well again he'll straighten out if he makes other friends, joins a club or something."

I have to speak up. "Mom's right about Jeremy," I say. "But he's not the only one who needs help. We all do."

"Angie!" Dad doesn't like this, but I continue.

"We're not a family. We're four people living in the same house. And it's the same with Debbie and Boyd and their parents. Don't you see? All of us are in Jeremy's poem." I close my eyes, thinking of the words. "We're 'the shadows no one wants to see, with screams no one wants to hear.' We're 'the ghosts of now.' Only I don't want to be a ghost, and neither does Jeremy."

They let me go to the hospital to see Jeremy, even though it's so late. I go alone. I don't even want Del to be with me.

The corridor is empty. My footsteps echo on the tiles. If anyone tries to make me leave, they'll be in for a fight. But I'm ignored. Mrs. Burrows is drinking a cup of coffee. I ask her to leave, and though I try to be polite, I suppose I sound so determined that she scurries from the room without a question.

It doesn't take long to go through the story with

Jeremy. But that's not what's important. What I need to tell him comes next.

"I'm your sister," I say, "and I love you. I love you so much that a lot of things I thought were important aren't any more. I'm going to live here and go to the junior college for the next two years. We may never make it as a real family, but if the two of us are together, then we can try."

I reach over and lightly touch the yellowed bruise on his forehead. "Jeremy," I say, "when you get right down to it, 'brother' and 'sister' is a big deal. It goes on forever." I gently squeeze his hand. "I'm glad I'm your sister."

At first I think Jeremy's long, gentle sigh must be from my imagination. But slowly, his hand barely turns and his fingers press steadily against mine.

THE END